THE LEGACY SERIES

SERIES TITLES

Shocker in Gloomtown
Dan Libman

American Animism
Jamey Gallagher

Keeping What's Best Left Kept Secret
David Ricchiute

Soaked
Toby LeBlanc

The Path of Totality: Stories & A Novella
Marie Zhuikov

The Continental Divide
Bob Johnson

The Three Devils and Other Stories
William Luvaas

The Correct Response
Manfred Gabriel

Welcome Back to the World: A Novella & Stories
Rob Davidson

Greyhound Cowboy and Other Stories
Ken Post

Close Call
Kim Suhr

The Waterman
Gary Schanbacher

Signs of the Imminent Apocalypse and Other Stories
Heidi Bell

What We Might Become
Sara Reish Desmond

The Silver State Stories
Michael Darcher

An Instinct for Movement
Michael Mattes

The Machine We Trust
Tim Conrad

Gridlock
Brett Biebel

Salt Folk
Ryan Habermeyer

The Commission of Inquiry
Patrick Nevins

Maximum Speed
Kevin Clouther

Reach Her in This Light
Jane Curtis

The Spirit in My Shoes
John Michael Cummings

*The Effects of Urban Renewal on Mid-Century America and
Other Crime Stories*
Jeff Esterholm

"This collection shows true range: realism that's weightless, surrealism that's grounding, and a world of experience in between."

—AARON SITZE
author of *The Andrew Jackson Stories*

"With cutting wit and poignant observation, Dan Libman's stories deliver a reading experience that variously strokes and pokes the soft underbelly of our deepest wishes and vulnerabilities. Playful, inventive, and funny, *Shocker in Gloomtown* will crack you up and crack open a new line of sight into the absurdities of the human condition."

—JOSEPH O'MALLEY
author of *Great Escapes from Detroit*

"Dan Libman is equally dexterous rendering a fictional work in realism or fabulism, and likewise adroit in blurring the two seamlessly together, with the understated ironic perspective of a Coen Brothers film."

—CRIS MAZZA
author of *Various Men Who Knew Us as Girls*

Shocker
in
Gloomtown

stories

Dan Libman

Cornerstone Press, Stevens Point, Wisconsin 54481
Copyright © 2025 Dan Libman
www.uwsp.edu/cornerstone

Printed in the United States of America by
Point Print and Design Studio, Stevens Point, Wisconsin

Library of Congress Control Number: 2024948515
ISBN: 978-1-960329-73-8

Cornerstone Press titles are produced in courses and internships offered by the
Department of English at the University of Wisconsin–Stevens Point.

DIRECTOR & PUBLISHER
Dr. Ross K. Tangedal

EXECUTIVE EDITORS
Jeff Snowbarger, Freesia McKee

EDITORIAL DIRECTOR
Brett Hill

SENIOR EDITOR
Ellie Atkinson

PRESS STAFF
Cora Bender, Madalyn Carpenter, Mai Kao Hang, Lillian Kulbeck, Allison Lange,
Sophie McPherson, Christiana Niedzwiecki, Eva Nielsen, Hannah Rouer, Madison
Schultz, Ava Willett

For my mom

ALSO BY DAN LIBMAN:

Book of Grudges
Married but Looking

Stories

Charon's Kayak

My dad's wife asked my brother and me to think of anecdotes to tell at his funeral. I was sketching one out, pencil to napkin, at Breakers Saloon when Mitch came in to see if I wanted some hours. He's about fifteen years younger than me and throws me a couple of shifts mid-week at his river rafting business if the teenagers are otherwise engaged riding skateboards or getting high. It doesn't matter what I'm wearing, Mitch has extra "staff" t-shirts and one pair of flip-flops a customer left behind. I like spending summer afternoons putting canoes and kayaks in the water, making sure life preservers are snug, warning newbies about the strong currents after the railroad bridge. I'm good with the chitchat, *You folks going to stay in town for dinner? Alfano's makes a pretty mean lasagna. If you like wings, Chili Pepper Cafe is the place to go.* I'll wrap up the day hosing off the kayaks and paddleboards and putting life vests back in plastic tubs. It's physical and sometimes hard, but I enjoy standing in the water at our launch site behind the old Conover Piano Factory. Our spot is slightly shady from the canopy of old growth pines and you can actually hear the river babbling off in the distance. The sound is steady and warm like a party. I feel like I'm sending customers out to float toward some great celebration that I haven't been invited to.

When the day is over Mitch escorts me back to Breakers, though it's just a few blocks and I can easily walk myself. Because Mitch is married and his wife likes him, he doesn't get to be in the bar as much as me and I can tell he's always a little excited to be there. He likes to ask Vic "what's on tap" even though it never changes. Last time he went over and got a wax tub of popcorn for us. I had never seen anyone eat the popcorn at Breakers before. Mitch took a swallow and centered his glass on the coaster. He glanced at my napkin which Vic had left for me from the morning. I had only written, "Dad was . . ."

"Real sorry about your father," Mitch said, not for the first time. "Burying a dad must be tough."

I told him, "His wife is paying some other guys to do it. All I have to do is fly in and say something."

Mitch's dad had died young and was probably a pretty good guy judging by how Mitch turned out. My dad had made it far enough in life to get a whole new family going, and I had a group of steps whom I was a lot older than and didn't know much about.

Mitch checked his watch. I knew he would only have two beers before going home. That was his rule for making sure he didn't turn into an alcoholic. One time one of the rafters called me a drunk because I was unsteady on my feet when I put her son on the river. I corrected her, "Not an alcoholic; emotionally dependent." I can go days without a beer and sometimes I even do. That's my rule. Not being an alcoholic is all about making rules—having a line—and then not crossing it. For example, Mitch won't have more than two beers *and* he won't drink before 5pm, even in the summer. Sometimes we pick up a group of rafters at the landing-site and they're in a great mood and still have a couple of cans left, so they'll offer us a beer while we're strapping the canoes to the trailer. If it's before five, Mitch will decline. Me, I think it's bad luck to not drink a beer someone else paid for.

FOR THE FUNERAL, I met my brother Russ in Houston. We hadn't seen each other in person for years but we shared a hotel room, and his wife, Prudence, arranged for his flight to land at about the same time as mine. Her idea was that we could split cab fare and save money, but somehow I ended up renting a car when I bought my plane ticket, because I was using the small screen on my phone. It had to do with a package deal that I thought I was only reading about but somehow had agreed to when all the clicking was done. I had a driver's license but hadn't owned a car since my divorce.

On the flight, I worked on the anecdotes my dad's wife had asked for. My father had only ever given me two pieces of advice, both bad. The first, when I was fifteen and he was teaching me to drive, was to hide a twenty behind my driver's license to bribe the cop if I got pulled over. "Don't even say anything. They just take the money and you go."

The second piece of advice came when he married the woman he was cheating on my mom with. I was almost thirty at the time but he told me I had to be his best man. I knew standing up at the wedding would be betraying my mother, but I went ahead and did it anyway because it was easier than saying no. He sent me a plane ticket and the advice he gave me was to be sure I demanded the *full* can of Coke on the flight. "They'll try to give you a plastic cup with half the pop. Don't take it."

I knew those would make poor funeral anecdotes so I let Russ speak for our family—my dad's first family—even though Russ was younger by almost five years. Russ was nervous, but he had the foresight to wear a tie and get a haircut. I was wearing a t-shirt, but I had a sports coat over it that I was surprised to find in my closet. As long as I didn't try to button it, the coat looked fine. I had bought it at Goodwill just a couple of years ago and had worn it when I got married, which we did at city hall by ourselves. My mother and dad weren't able to be in the same room with each other back then, and Vanessa's family weren't much better. The marriage was over within a year anyway. I hadn't worn the jacket since.

Russ and I stood next to each other at the church, and I kept my head bowed—somberly, I hoped—as Russ mentioned a couple of family vacations we took and that dad was "good in a crisis," the one to call if you got into a car accident. Russ kind of mumbled—I had trouble hearing some of it and I was standing right next to him. The step-kids did a lot better, even though my dad wasn't their real father, they seemed genuinely broken up. My stepbrother recited a poem he found online and had some trouble reading off his phone because his hand was shaking. His sister managed to get choked up during her anecdote, which actually *was* about my dad helping her after a motorcycle accident, just like Russ had said. I thought that was a bit of a coincidence, but no one remarked upon it, not even Russ. When it was over, he whispered, "Hope that was okay," and I told him he did fine, considering the material he was working with was kind of on the challenging side. He could have told some pretty hairy stories. When my dad told us he was leaving my mother to be with Kay, he assured me and Russ that everything was mutual, and he and mother had made an agreement to never say an ill word about each other. Dad may even have been under the impression she honored that agreement.

Russ and I skipped the after-party and went to a Friday's and had dinner. I would have liked a beer but didn't want to drink in front of Russ because he was in the program. Since I have that rule about being able to go some days without a drink, it wasn't a big deal, although, as it turned out, Russ was on his phone a lot texting Prue so a beer would have been good company. Russ and Prue had a nice relationship and sometimes I wondered if I had a little bit of a crush on her. Prue had yellow hair like the girls in Archie comics and she was efficient and good with schedules. She was the one who told me which flight to get and even offered to buy my ticket. I didn't know if she meant *pay for* my ticket and to avoid the awkwardness I did it myself, which worked out fine except for ending up with the rental car. I also liked Mitch's wife and I liked Bonnie who was married to Vic, the guy who owns Breakers. I tend to develop crushes on all my friends' wives. Sometimes I think it's because it's safe to pine for them and sometimes I think crushing on my friends wives is a way of expressing something about how I feel for my male friends, but those are the kind of thoughts that only come to me before beer-thirty, when I'm harder on myself.

The TV wasn't working in the hotel room Prue got Russ and me, but he started scrolling on his phone anyway, trying to find a meeting. He said Dad's funeral had been tough for him, but he could tell I was in "a different place." I didn't react to that. An app told him of a meeting not too far away, but he would need a ride. I still had my keys in my pocket and we headed out.

"Maybe you'd find it interesting to attend with me," Russ said when I pulled out of the lot. "When they go around the room, say you're there for support."

I pointed out I was wearing a Bud Light t-shirt.

"Lots of them will be wearing beer shirts. It's not like you get a new wardrobe when you start the program."

Just then, some guy came on the radio and said he wanted to dedicate a song to his deceased father. He identified himself as Mike from Arkansas and said his dad had been gone fifteen years but he still thought about him, "literally every day." My dad had only been dead a week and a couple times on the plane I had to remind myself why I was flying to Houston. If I thought about him at all it was along the lines of: man, in the end, he really got away with it.

The meeting was in the basement of a church and Russ knew to go to the back door even though he had never been to this meeting before, never been to Houston. Seemed like they had just started but we got two seats in the middle of a long table of men and women drinking coffee which I could smell was pretty burnt. They were going around saying how long they'd been sober. It didn't matter the length, thirty years or thirty hours, everyone got a round of applause. I said, "I'm just here to support my brother," as Russ had coached me, which I assumed was the same as "skip me" but everyone clapped anyway. One guy said I was a "good man." I didn't feel like a good man, and I immediately wished I hadn't said "just" before saying "here to support." Russ said we were from out of town and he had four years of sobriety and had come to this meeting because this was the first major tragedy he had gone through sober. I was genuinely surprised to hear our dad's death being described as a tragedy, let alone a "major" one.

The steady drip of coincidences—my stepsister telling a story about a crisis and the guy on the radio talking about his dad—now turned into a gusher. A woman talked about *her* dad who was dead, though she herself was old and her father had died many years before. She said she was just thinking about her dad for no reason. And then another guy was talking about death, not his dad's, but he was wearing a White Sox cap. Our dad was a huge White Sox fan. Pretty much all I talked about with him during the last few years of his life was the White Sox and why they weren't good anymore after going all the way in '05.

On the way back to the hotel, Russ said he was grateful I had come with, which I already knew because he had said it to the group. I asked, "Did you notice all the weird coincidences? Like the lady with her dad and the White Sox guy?"

"What White Sox guy?"

"The guy with the White Sox cap? Dad's favorite team."

"Were they?" Russ said, "People tend to find meaning where they need to find meaning. I remember thinking that way at the start of my program, that no matter what anyone said, they were really speaking about my experience. You should pay attention to that feeling. Maybe think about it later."

He was texting while talking and then the red and blues of a police car throbbed in my mirror. I was being pulled over. I thought about the twenty my dad said I should have in my wallet for cops and I was going to say something about it to Russ, *how about that for another coincidence*, but the cop rolled past. He was pulling someone else over. But how could that just happen, that I almost got pulled over the same day I was thinking about Dad's advice?

Our flights were early and he called Prue on his cell, so to give him a little space I walked across the street to a bar called Chump Change and had a beer. My plan was to call my mother and tell her about the funeral, but I wasn't in the mood to talk to her boyfriend if he answered. I ordered a Busch Light and rested my phone on the polished bar. Russ once told me that my mother had taken him aside and apologized to him for not being "there enough" for him when he was younger. My mother said, according to Russ, that she spent all her energy protecting me from dad, who was still something of a hitter when I was a little kid. I don't remember much of the "protecting," although she did make my dad go to therapy, and something called "The Managing Your Anger Workbook" eventually made its way to a bookshelf in our den. And as far as I know, Russ never had a plate of food broken over his head for talking back at dinner, and I doubt any of my step siblings ever got body-slammed and had their ribs kicked for throwing a football that knocked off the old man's glasses.

The bartender brought me a second beer and I thought Chump Change was just my kind of bar: lively but not too aggressive, a solid rail for your feet at just the right height, a bartender who calls you honey and pays attention to where you're at with your beer. At one point, an older couple actually danced to a cowboy song on the jukebox. They did a showy little spin and she bent into a creaky dip before they were both reaching for their stools again. The place clapped for them anyway. I was figuring what to say to my mother, spinning my phone with one hand and working my beer with the other. It had felt for years like whenever we talked there was some irritating subject we were always avoiding. Things would be easier between us now, but I wasn't so sure about me and Russ. It seemed possible that without Dad, Russ and I wouldn't have anything in common anymore. I would miss Prue. As far as my dad went, I decided to officially say goodbye by demanding the full cup of Coke on the plane ride home.

SOME OLD NEIGHBORS, the Mendelssohns, came by the Rock River Rafters. "Your father and I," he said while clasping the XXL life preserver across his massive belly. "We used to say we were the only ones in the subdivision with jobs. I saw your dad every morning. He'd be going to the bank just as I was heading out to the shop. We were probably the only guys who set an alarm. How's he doing?"

I told him my dad was fine and helped him get in the canoe. Mr. Mendelssohn was huge, and his wife was even bigger, but I let her hold my arm and used all my strength to keep the canoe from tipping.

Mr. and Mrs. Mendelssohn paddled into the current just as I had told them to, and I saw him put the paddle back into the canoe and settle in for the ride. Their bodies shifted as they slid toward the dappled sunlight. From the launch site, I can see the exact moment when our customers stop being nervous about the river and accept the ride; their bodies settle, tension leaves their shoulders.

It wasn't until they got past the riverbend that I remembered my dad was not fine, that he was dead. I wasn't mad at myself for having said the wrong thing, that sort of change takes some getting used to. It had seemed like Mr. Mendelssohn asked about the dad he knew, the one who drove off to work every morning, the dad I had when I was ten years old, and that dad was fine. The dad my stepbrothers and sisters had, the one whose death Russ described as a "major tragedy," that's who had died.

It felt strange just then—standing in the river looking at the distant ripples where the canoe had gone—to think about my dad being dead. Strange thinking about it, and also strange to notice myself thinking about it. Not the kind of thought I usually have, but as Russ suggested after his meeting, I paid attention to the feeling. I might even think about it later.

Hunt Club

The bicyclist takes two pills at night; one lowers the number on his daily blood pressure self-check, and the other is supposed to keep him from waking up to pee so much, but all it really seems to do is decrease the number of pumps he gets when ejaculating. He takes the pills right before bed because they make him dizzy.

Earlier at dinner, he had corrected his niece that the January Sixth commission wasn't a trial and then he corrected his wife that the co-chairperson's first name was Liz, not Lynn. They had gone to Hunt Club, a bar and grill boasting forty thousand dollars worth of taxidermy hanging from the rafters: bears and raccoons, claws out, teeth bared as though about to pounce and rip the diners to shreds. The cyclist was asked to leave the table "for a minute." The request coincided with a change in topic to the Supreme Court and the revocation of reproductive rights, and the cyclist thought they wanted to talk about his niece's birth control without him being around, but it may also have had to do with all the correcting he had been doing.

Usually Hunt Club was packed with locals drinking Busch Lights and eating cheeseburgers, but it was still a little early and there were plenty of open tables. The cyclist kept his head down and played Spelling Bee on his phone. His banishment went on for a lot longer than a minute and he wondered if he'd been forgotten, but he sure as hell wasn't about to ask if he could come back. Sometimes the cyclist could get to "Genius" on Spelling Bee, and he would take a screenshot and brag on the family thread. His kids would even sometimes put a heart on the photo, but then his son told him Genius wasn't actually the top level on Spelling Bee, there was something called "Queen Bee" which was a level beyond Genius. The cyclist had felt a profound, years long, retroactive shame. At Hunt Club he worked the puzzle, spun the tiles looking for words with the middle letter, *affirm affirming afar affair*, until his wife signaled he could come back to the table. The burgers had come and she had already taken two bites of his, having only ordered salad for herself.

That night the cyclist took his two pills and went to sleep. He dozed but a sound from the patch of scrubby weed trees outside the bedroom window startled them. It sounded like one of their chickens in great distress. He knew he had closed and locked their small chicken coop but maybe one bird hadn't gotten back yet? He and his wife shouted out through the screened window to scare off whatever was out there. It went quiet so they turned off the lights and—judging by the rhythmic breathing from the driver's side of the bed—his wife got back to sleep.

Hours later, the same sound woke them again: a terri-fied, strangled cry. They grabbed flashlights and boots and went outside to the edge of the timber. The cyclist found a streak of feathers in the lawn, which meant he had left a hen exposed and now it was being eaten. He had always assumed predators killed in seconds, but the torture had been going on all night. He and his wife couldn't see anything despite the flashlights and bright moon because the timber was so overgrown with branches and poison ivy. They peered over the propane tank and waved their flashlights but saw nothing except years of landscaping neglect.

It was after 4am now, and the cyclist certainly wouldn't be falling back asleep. His thoughts drifted back to dinner. While they ate, Hunt Club had filled with motorcycle riders because of the three day weekend, large men and women— they took up space these riders; their hair and their pirate costumes and their bellies and their loud voices. Each rider had a wife or girlfriend with him in matching studs and fringe. In the middle of the tumult, one woman had stood out. She was young and wore a white dress so tight she could not possibly have come with the pack of riders. Maybe she sat sidesaddle or in a sidecar, but she also seemed too clean. She and the bicyclist made eye contact for one second while he was alone playing Spelling Bee. Knowing his place in the world, he made sure to not catch her eye again, but he did steal a few quick glances. Her sleeveless dress revealed arms covered in delicate tattoos. Her skin held no tan and the blue ink made her look like an elaborate mahjong tile. The man she was with was the largest rider, tall and thick; he palmed her hip and she nestled under his arm and touched her lips to his neck. The cyclist wondered if she was being paid to spend the day with him because he was gawky and frankly unabashedly ugly. It was only *her* attention that gave him any kind of presence, and at some point, they had disappeared without the cyclist noticing.

There is nothing so pitiable as an old man awake at night thinking about a young woman, but he told himself what he felt was curiosity and not desire; interest, not heat. Her pristineness had been so out of place at Hunt Club, he wondered if he was remembering correctly, or maybe he had made her up. Still, it made him happy to be thinking of her. His blood pressure medication made his toes and fingers cold even on warm days. He used a heavier blanket and had taken to wearing slippers in the house. It was a comfort to think he could still notice a woman.

There was some pink coming through the blinds when the cyclist again heard noise: a muted, weak screech. The hen in her final moments making herself heard, a final cry into the void. It hadn't even woken his wife, and this time, he just stayed in bed and hoped the end would be merciful.

Basic Red Coffee Pot, the

Not by choice was Floyd Potinjur the first great explorer of 8am Rockford, Illinois, a brave cartographer of uncivilized lands. Floyd's son, Porter, was having trouble with Intro to Calculus and his teacher had found him a tutor who took students for an hour at a time in the breakfast nook of his ranch home on Mulford near State, but he was only available early Sunday mornings, "before church." Inconvenient to be sure, but necessary as the lad really seemed to be struggling. There was no shame in it: Floyd himself had some ability with Math but had failed three times at Beginning Spanish: once in middle school, again freshman year of high school and finally one last desperate shot in college. (There was even a fourth attempt, but that was night school in a continued learning program which he undertook "for fun" but stopped going—not because he couldn't figure it out, but because it turned out he had other stuff going on.) Each successive attempt at Beginning Spanish would be easier than the last: he would fly through early vocabulary: *lapiz, mesa, vase de agua*, he would get the taste of a tense: I, we, you, you all, you familiar. . . . Floyd would be on autopilot, cruising effortlessly until reaching something new, something he hadn't encountered in his last try: an irregular verb, a subjunctive case, and he would summarily crash and burn. How then could he get mad at Porter for having trouble with Math? Instead, he sleepily packed both kids in the car and drove from Belvedere to "The Forest City."

Three stores were open early Sundays and Floyd usually picked one to take his daughter to while Porter worked with the tutor, but the third weekend in November, air just starting to bite, Floyd pulled the first hat trick of the Intro to Calculus season, hitting all three in search for a coffee maker. The Mister Coffee Basic had begun brewing powdery sludge along with the coffee. Rather than clean it, his wife Marilyn decided to sink the thirty-five bucks into a new one.

"We don't have any vinegar anyway, just get a new pot Sunday. Don't look at me like that, Floydsy, I don't even drink it."

Marilyn had quit coffee when Yoga Glossy fingered caffeine as a source of flatulence during various sphincter squeezing stretches—particularly Warrior Pose—reducing her three cup habit down to sipping from his mug when Floyd's back was turned.

"I don't need coffee anymore. I get a lift just grinding the beans and watching you drink yours." She handed him a mug with a moist blob on the rim where her lips had been. Since that time, Marilyn developed an attitude about women who farted throughout Advanced Yoga. "Bernice is like a Howitzer from *om* to *namaste*—I can tell what she had for breakfast."

"So I'm buying a new coffee pot?"

"Yes," Marilyn said. "Exactly like this. Only red to match the toaster."

THEY BEGAN AT THE HOME DEPOT where he and Kiya careened up and down the wide, empty aisles, Floyd swerving recklessly and Kiya hanging on the front of the cart like a backward maiden on a ship. She was eight years old and her winter boots were pink and filthy, and Floyd wished she had removed her mittens so she could grip tighter.

Shopping in the Home Depot was like buying rocks in a mountain range: so much product on a scale so grossly inhuman that it made Floyd giddy. He could have gone right to the appliances but he knew to go slow, to deliberate: sixty minutes was an awful long time in a Rockford morning. Pacing was something he had learned as an apprentice plumber: when in someone's warm kitchen—on the clock—and working a cushy hairball in the pipes, you were kind of just acting against your own interests to finish the job quickly. There was always another dispatch at the end of a work order and the next one might mean reaching into someone's septic or fighting rats in an unfinished crawl space.

Kiya was laughing, hanging tight for dear life as Floyd took a wide turn near the registers. While buzzing an endcap of multicolored duct tape for the girl's amusement, one of the cashiers, a spindly older woman more orange vest than torso, raised her voice.

"Sir, they'd rather you didn't let children ride on the carts! Sir!"

The next way station in 8am Rockford was Target, where everything was bright and happy and tidy and orderly and clean, and where Kiya could not be coaxed back on the front of a cart.

"Because of what they said in the last store?" Floyd asked her.

"No." Kiya hooked her mittened pinky around a wire in the shopping cart and walked glumly alongside, her mud-caked boots working as a kind of civil disobedience against the gleam of the floor.

"Kiya, that cashier was a joy stomper. The only way to combat joy stomping is to not allow your joy to be stomped. Get on the cart."

"I just don't want to ride anymore."

Occasionally, he had seen his daughter reduced to tears because he or Marilyn had forgotten to sign her homework the night before and then Kiya would have to "flip her card" and if she did that enough times, she would miss an outdoors recess. For Kiya, just flipping the card was devastating enough: she simply didn't like to get in trouble. She would leave the room during a Beaver rerun if Ward so much as raised an eyebrow toward the boys, and when she was little she couldn't stand the page in *Cat in the Hat* where the fish announces that the mother is coming. Kiya would leap off the arm of the Gentle Brown Chair and beg for him to skip to the next page, even when they had read the book many times and knew everything would turn out fine. And he always discussed with her the question posed by the children at the end of the book:

> *Should we tell her about it?*
> *Now what SHOULD we do?*
> *Well...*
> *What would you do*
> *If your mother asked YOU?*

"Even if I knew I would get in trouble, I would tell a grown up," Floyd would pointedly say. "Because that's the right thing to do, right Kiya? You must always tell a grownup, right Kiya? No matter what."

Sometimes Kiya would agree that telling a grownup was the right thing to do without actually saying she would tell the grown up, and sometimes she sat silent, resentful about being spun in such a ham-handed way.

Target had coffee makers but not red ones. Floyd still had twenty-five minutes left.

Stop number three, Kohl's, he generally avoided because Kohl's depressed him. Shopping at Kohl's was like eating lunch at a Subway, something he only did if he couldn't get back home and all other options were exhausted. If Floyd was eating at Subway, it was only because Every Single Plan he had made for himself that day had gone awry. Subway was lunch for beginners, sandwiches for people who knew their bodies required fuel but had no interest in food, just as Kohl's was shopping for people who needed goods but didn't care what those goods looked like. On the drive over, Floyd had considered various ways of coaxing Kiya up for a ride again, but the Kohl's shopping cart was more a rolling mesh hanging from an aluminum skeleton, and it seemed like it might actually be dangerous. But Floyd did have success in the House Wares section.

"You took a red one," Kiya pointed out. They were in line at the register and Floyd remembered he hadn't taken Marilyn's charge card, which meant that he wasn't going to get a scratch-off for a possible discount, which was fine with him because he found the whole charade tedious and undignified.

"I know, sweetie. I meant to get a red one."

But it did mean he was going to have the same conversation again about not wanting a Kohl's credit card because his family already had one, and no, the cashier couldn't look it up for him because it was under his wife's last name, and yes, he knew he could get one too, and yes, he knew opening an account would mean ten percent off the forty dollars for the coffee maker on top of whatever mystery discount he might get from the scratch-off (har har), but nevertheless, he didn't want a Kohl's credit card, and no, he didn't have a good reason. He just didn't want one.

"But the coffee pot at home is black, Daddy."

"I know."

"Mom might," she swallowed, "be mad."

"Change is good. Did Daddy ever tell you about all the trouble he had learning Beginning Spanish?"

She nodded.

"My first year at a going away college, a sleep over college which I didn't get to go to until my third year because of financial issues, I decided that I had washed out in Beginning Spanish so often, I should try a new language. I picked Beginning Italian because it's close to Beginning Spanish."

Floyd was happy to be distracted from the spectacle of the crone in front of him fishing a coin from her wallet to scratch her discount game card.

"But what happened was that it was so close to Beginning Spanish, it hindered the language acquisition process—the learning—and it made things harder. I dropped out in a week."

"Oh dear," the woman sweetly sighed, pushing the card back to the cashier. "It says not this time."

Kiya asked, "Was this at Rock Valley Community?"

"No no, this was my semester at Rockford College."

"When did you go to plumber school?"

"Mmmm. . . . Right around the time I dropped Beginning Italian. I do remember one Italian phrase. *Dopodomani*. That means day after tomorrow." He put on a movie accent and gestured broadly with his wrist. "*Do. . . po. . . domani*."

The cashier was ready for them. "May I see your Kohl's card?"

THAT EVENING MARILYN CLEANED the kitchen because Thanksgiving was coming up and it was their turn to host, which meant Floyd cleaned the fridge, tossing out all the sour creams now green, marveling again at another army of quarter-filled salsa jars while calling out to the family that he didn't understand how "things had gotten so bad again." He put the old, black Mister Coffee Basic into the Hefty bag and took it all to the subdivision's dumpster.

As he was unpacking the new coffee pot, raising the Styrofoam sarcophagus, Marilyn reached around and removed the glass pot. "I really like the red handle," she said and then turned to hold it next to the red toaster, bobbled it, lost her grip on the clear packaging, and dropped it to the kitchen floor where it shattered mess free, still in the shipping bag.

"Sorry." She held up the bag of broken glass like a pet store goldfish.

"It's okay." He grumbled to let her know he was irritated.

"Just bring it back to Kohl's tomorrow and say it was already broken."

He was about to say something about the receipt when Kiya ran in the kitchen from the living room looking horrified. "You're not allowed to do that!"

Floyd lowered his head and Marilyn chuckled. "Big stores always take stuff back when something's wrong. It's the cost of doing business."

"She's right, Mom," Porter came up behind her using his brand new, big boy voice. "Nothing was wrong, you broke it. It's not right."

"We're joking," Floyd muttered. "Your mother was joking. A private joke about something that happened before we were *blessed* with you two."

Marilyn turned. "Maybe the old coffee pot will fit. They're both Basics, right? It won't have the red handle. . . ."

Floyd shook his head. "In the dumpster."

Marilyn winked sweetly toward Porter and Kiya. "I'll get a new one tomorrow," she said. "And Floyd, you can drive through a Mickey D for caffeine."

"Fine," he said. "But what are you going to do for coffee?"

"I don't drink coffee anymore."

THE NEXT MORNING FLOYD DROVE through Dunkee D for coffee which threw his timing off, and he had to use the bathroom at a customer's house, something all plumbers are told to avoid if at all possible. He was eager to set up the new pot that evening and asked Marilyn where it was.

"Didn't get to go shopping," she told him. "But tomorrow morning I'm going to be near a Kohl's, not the one you went to in Rockford, but the one in DeKalb on Sycamore because I have a temp job at Kresler's Travel Agency. I've temped there before and no one ever calls so I can sneak across the street and get it. Remind me to bring my charge so I can get a discount card!"

On Tuesday morning, Floyd had another Dunkin coffee and came home for lunch. He asked where the new coffee maker was.

"I didn't have time," Marilyn said handing him a sandwich. "I had to get a pencil case for Porter at that college bookstore and old man Kresler was in the office all afternoon."

In the late afternoon Marilyn did Yoga in the basement and then took a long bath. Floyd let himself get angry. *She broke it, she said she'd get another one, she didn't, then she didn't, and still she won't. How was it she was holding out without coffee? Exercise? No way!* He went to her car, sure to find a Starbucks cup so he could storm into the bathroom. *Aha!* he'd say. All he found in the cup holder was her cell phone, and even that promising flash-point dissolved because it was still half charged. He took the phone and plugged it in and then went into the bathroom and said to the smoked glass, with as much importance as he could muster, "You forgot to recharge your phone but I brought it in and plugged it in for you." Her response, "Thanks," was far less a provocation than he'd hoped for.

THEY ATE STIR FRY FOR DINNER, just vegetables and no chicken since they were so close to Thanksgiving. Porter and Kiya made themselves peanut butter sandwiches because Porter didn't like chicken and Kiya didn't like broccoli, and even though the dish had neither offending item, the kids insisted that since they always made sandwiches on stir fry night, that's what they wanted to do now. Still, the combination of Porter glopping enough peanut butter onto his bread for eight sandwiches and Kiya nervously arranging the napkin on her lap, plus the decrease in his caffeine intake—made him unable to hold back.

"We're just making the same mistakes over and over again. Same mistakes, family Potinjur! We break something, we don't replace it. We want salsa, we open a new jar, we never check if there already is an open jar of salsa. We eat. . . . messy! I ever tell you about the Beginner's Spanish Dictionary?"

"The dots, Dad?" Porter asked while chewing.

Marilyn scooped a blob of peanut butter off the table with her hand and wiped it back into the jar.

"On my third go-round with Beginner's Spanish I bought a new dictionary thinking that a change in books might inspire me to do better. I was so enthusiastic that I decided I would put a little black dot next to each word I looked up. I would make these dots and then at the end of the course when I moved on to Intermediate Spanish, I would fan the dictionary and see all the black dots and it would be a visual representation of what I learned, each dot a Spanish word I had mastered. So I sat down on the first day of class with my new dictionary and my worksheet, and there was a question with a word that I didn't know. I looked it up in my new dictionary and got the English meaning, and I took my pencil and put my first black dot next to the Spanish word. I answered the question on my worksheet, got to my second question, and there was another word that I didn't know. So I took my Spanish dictionary, and there next to the new word I was looking up was a black dot." He paused to let it sink in. "It was the same word. We're just spinning our wheels, Marilyn, making the same mistakes over and over again."

He watched Porter reaching for another set of bread slices while Kiya chewed her potato chips. She was counting chews. No one said anything and when Marilyn realized he was looking at her she smiled at him kindly, the way a kindergarten teacher smiles at a kid who has drawn a picture for her.

"My head is throbbing," Floyd told her. "We need to get a working coffee pot. Soon."

They had sex that night, and it was sweet and easy, even though when Marilyn took her knees and raised her legs, it occurred to him that she was maybe practicing some yoga position: stacking chores, the same way she did the dishes while talking to her sister on the phone. In fact, as he got more frenzied, he thought he could detect that her breathing was regulated. She was counting: inhale one two three, hold it one two three, exhale one two three. . . He could recall Denise Austin calling for just that exact rhythm on the Denise Austin's *25 Minute Iyengar Yoga Workout DVD* Marilyn watched. He decided to keep thinking about Denise Austin in her yoga clothes.

When they were done he asked, "You come?"

"Yep. Nice n' tingly, lots of waves. You?"

"Yeah. Real good."

"I can tell you haven't masturbated for a while."

"Ha ha, Marilyn."

"Must be busy at work."

"Ha ha. Oh, by the way: *namaste*."

"What?"

"Nothing."

"Why did you say that?

"No reason. Good night."

THEY AWOKE WHEN KIYA OPENED the bedroom door and padded over to Marilyn's side. "Mom," she said. "Mom. Mom."

When Marilyn got the table lamp on, they found Kiya holding a book.

"Mom. Do you really want to be a giraffe?"

"What now," Marilyn croaked.

"In the book it's what you said." She opened an old Dr. Seuss *My Book about Me,* the one Marilyn had written in as a child. With a blunt orange crayon Kiya pointed to where Marilyn had checked the box referring to Giraffes.

Marilyn grunted. "Hmmm. . . . I guess not. The book only gives you a couple of choices."

"Then I'm going to cross out your mistake."

Floyd stirred. "No honey. The book represents what Mom thought when she was little."

"Did you ever have blonde hair mom? Mom? Not to offend you, but did you ever have blonde hair? Why did you color your hair like this?"

Before Floyd could stop her, Kiya darkened with a black crayon the orange and yellow hair Marilyn had drawn when she was a child. He got up to use the bathroom and shower and by the time he was finished, everyone had settled into the kitchen. He went to the coffee pot before remembering. He knew to not show anger—that was sort of the unspoken deal if they had sex, Floyd had to go a certain amount of time without a flare up. Otherwise, *Gee,* she would say, *I would have thought under the circumstances you would be in a better mood this morning. Guess I'll have to remember that the next time you come a-knockin.* No work the day before Thanksgiving, no excuse to drive through anywhere and he refused the black tea she offered him on principle, though he noted with some satisfaction Marilyn was gulping hers down with some urgency.

Floyd's parents flew in from Sarasota and the Potinjurs met them at Rockford International, Kiya bouncing on her heels with excitement. Even Porter wasn't too old to get worked up by a visit from Minnsie and Poppsy.

"Long flight, Floydsy." Poppsy was shaky but could still hoist Kiya for a wet raspberry on her neck. "We should eat something before mother has a blood sugar issue. Close and easy. A Subway sandwich or something would be fine."

Floyd licked his lips, wrestled with his crabbiness, which seemed to have him in a sleeper hold: he could hear the ref counting. "Do you ever get tired of suggesting the same stupid restaurant over and over? If Subway can even be classified as a restaurant."

Poppsy put his hands up comically, signaling *what's wrong with this guy?* Porter busted up, thrilled to be in on the joke.

His mother ruffled Floyd's hair. "Sounds like someone didn't get enough coffee this morning."

Marilyn ruffled the other side of Floyd's head. "It's my fault because I dropped—"

"We'll go to Potbelly." Floyd shook them all loose. "It's like Subway but a little better. Just slightly."

"YOU WERE KIND OF HARD on your dad back there," Marilyn said once the kids had been settled into the backseat of his parent's rental. Floyd checked the mirror to make sure they were following and could see them all having an animated conversation, having fun. Floyd slowly led them through the intersection.

"Doesn't anyone want to get any better at anything?" he said calmly, resisting the urge to spin in his seat and lash out, recognizing the impulse was nearly 60% caffeine related. Maybe 55%. "We're all just going to be content making the same ten mistakes every single day?"

"Suggesting Subway over Potbelly isn't a capital offense. You're too picky." Marilyn raised up in her seat, stiffened her spine, lined her shoulders together, hung her arms as best she could, and took a deep breath. "Try to find an. . . . equanimity, Floydsy. With life."

Weekday at 12:30pm Rockford was so different from Sunday morning Rockford that seeing it was almost excruciating, like looking at the burning bush. All the stores were open and the parking lots were full. Floyd had to stand in line for the sandwiches while Porter held a table. When they finished eating, Marilyn collected all the wrappers and cups and shoved it into the garbage. The kids returned to the back seat of his parent's rental, tussling for the position behind the driver.

"Marilyn and I have to get a new coffee pot," Floyd told his dad. "Porter knows where the key is hidden."

Marilyn directed Floyd to drive back to the strip mall with the Kohl's. He asked, "Did you bring your Kohl's card?"

"Oh shoot! Know what?" Marilyn pointed forward. "There's a Bed Bath and Beyond right in the same mall. Would this be less painful for you if we made the purchase in a different store?"

"Maybe," he conceded. "Did you bring one of those 10% coupons Bed Bath and Beyond always send?"

"I think so." Marilyn opened the glove box. "Mmmm. No. I thought you were going to put some in the glove box so that—"

"I told you to put some in the car."

"Do me a favor. You stay in the car. I'll come get you when I'm done. Try not to talk to anyone until we get some coffee made."

INSTEAD, FLOYD PACED on the narrow sidewalk even though it was clearly only intended for people to cross from the parking lot to the stores, not to stroll on horizontally. If Floyd squinted, he could make out an office supply wholesaler where he could get a new ink cartridge for the family printer, only he hadn't thought to bring the old one which he could get refilled cheaper. Or he could walk back into the lot and try and find a Starbucks. Or he could go to Target. Or he could—

When his phone began buzzing in his hand, he realized he had been standing still, staring into space, lost. He wasn't sure for how long.

"Floyd! They sell replacement pots in the Bed Bath and Beyond. They don't have red but we can get another black one; they're only fifteen dollars. Come quick, I'm nearly at the register and I don't have my Visa."

When he stepped through the sliding doors Marilyn was already handing the replacement pot to the cashier. He took out his credit card, and couldn't help himself, was unable to not tell the cashier, "We have one of those ten percent coupons, but not with us."

She was a young woman with a whole slew of novelty buttons on her vest. "Bring the receipt back and we'll prorate—"

Floyd cut her off. "I know. Because I always forget to bring the coupons, I know I can come back with the receipt. But I won't actually do it."

"You'd be surprised at how often people say they will and then don't come back."

Floyd couldn't swipe the card, which he held perched right at the lip of the magnetic chute. His coffee headache was tremendous, possibly causing the dark spots now swimming in his vision.

"So then. . . ." he said quietly. "Bed Bath and Beyond acknowledges that everyone on the planet has a coupon. Why not then just take the ten percent off now instead of making me go through the charade of going home, finding the damn thing, bringing it back—"

Marilyn pushed his hand and the machine dinged its approval of the sale.

"Let's get you home and try out the new pot," she said.

OUTSIDE THE KITCHEN WINDOW his father pitched a ball to Kiya, who swung wildly. Porter was catching and he had to chase after the wild pitch. Even his mother was planted with an old mitt near a pizza box being used for second base. Marilyn sat across from him with two matching coffee mugs. Her t-shirt said PORN STAR and Floyd felt happy to be with her. In fact, as he took his first sip, his tongue absorbing the coffee like a neglected house plant, he thought he loved Marilyn more that he could express. She was telling a story.

"At the travel agency on Tuesday, this guy called and said some other word for what they speak in Spain. I'm like, I'm pretty sure they speak Spanish in Spain."

Floyd held the coffee in his mouth, rolled it around, swallowed it. "Castilian," he said.

"Oh! That *is* what he called it. Don't tell me that guy was right! I thought he was nuts."

"They speak Castilian in Spain. But you were right too, because Castilian is Spanish."

"You're so smart," Marilyn said. "And thanks for trying to not make me feel bad. I appreciate that too. Aren't they being cute out there? Playing ball in this weather."

Floyd basked in her compliment. His wife thought he was smart, what could be better than that? But he felt uneasy about it suddenly. He was a fraud. He only knew those things about Spain because he had failed Beginning Spanish so many times. He wasn't smart at all. He only knew what he knew because he had failed at so many things so many times.

True, he was lucky to enjoy his job. He loved plumbing really, the feeling of coming to someone's house and being so needed, changing a homeowner's panic into relief just because he could do something they couldn't. But he was only a plumber because he had washed out of college. And he had let his parents down, especially his dad who wanted him to be a lawyer like he was, and even had to pull some strings just to get him into trade school. He had met Marilyn while drunk in a bar and while he loved his kids, he occasionally wondered what would have happened in his life if he hadn't gotten her pregnant early. And here she was saying he was smart and kind, and Floyd knew he was neither of those things, even though he wished he were. He had the urge to confess suddenly, a powerful, weepy desire to tell Marilyn he loved her. He loved her but he was a failure and dumb and nothing special at all and then beg for her forgiveness. It was right there, this confession, but he held back a moment.

Should he tell her about it? Now, what should he do? Well, what would you do if your wife thought that about you?

Bottomless Coffee, Topless Dancers

I first heard about my cousin's impending life implosion at a strip club in Rockford. I had just gotten a private lap dance from a woman who had pushed my knees apart, sat in my lap, and pressed her chest into my face. All the lap dances were done in a carpeted alcove that still smelled like cigarettes though it had been illegal to smoke indoors for years. In the area next to mine there was a guy in a wheelchair and when he finished getting his dance, my stripper, Roxy, had to skooch in to give him enough space to get past. She pressed tightly in a non-calculated way, and I helped her keep balanced by holding her at the waist—more intimate than usual—when the chair caught one of her discarded shoes. *Scuuze me*, she called after him. *Hey, Roy! Roy!* He couldn't hear her over the music. She rolled her eyes and we waited for him to get past so she could hop out of my lap and go after her shoe which the chair was still dragging across the floor. By the time she returned, the song had ended and neither one of us knew what we were supposed to do. *Did you want another dance*, she asked even though I hadn't really gotten a full one. I don't think she was cheating me—Roy had just gotten us off-track. *Same thing?* I said. I always asked because sometimes, after you paid for the first dance the girl might let you know that things could get friendlier. Roxy just shrugged which I couldn't interpret so I took out my wallet and said, *you're really good at this*, mostly as a way of having something to say while counting out the money. Roxy really lit up at the compliment. *I just love dancing,* she said. *I don't care what kind of dancing it is. It just makes me happy.* I knew her whole story just from that line.

"You would love the girls we hire at the store," my cousin said when Roxy walked me back to my seat. He was eyeing her as she walked away. Drew was drinking Diet Coke because he was in AA and he was also texting someone who I was pretty sure was the girl he'd shown me nude photos of on his phone. "Tall to reach over the counter," he continued. "Just your type." I hadn't gotten the dance from Roxy because she was necessarily my type, but because she had come over and asked me. I felt honored when a dancer came to me and hurt when they picked other guys to hustle.

Drew and I were the same age and had been close as children, hated each other in high school, but ended up being buddies again as adults. He was back in his phone and I was watching the next act but also keeping an eye on Roxy. For Drew, AA had been a preemptive strike. He had acknowledged a problem, alcoholism, and announced he was quitting. He had not acknowledged the pills, the check kiting, the girlfriends, or the embezzlement. That same year Drew lost both his pharmacies, his house, and all his money. What he hadn't lost was his wife, who vindictively stuck with him through it all. She sold the house while he was in rehab and moved to Naperville with her parents. When he got out of rehab, he had nowhere else to go but under her father's roof. He went to meetings every day and eventually got a job at a Walmart pharmacy, but under strict supervision due to his status as a recovering addict. Most of our relatives said Drew had gotten off easy, that he was lucky to have a good woman. It may even be the story he told himself.

AROUND THIS SAME TIME, I had another friend who dried up on me. His name was Josh and he was really the husband of one of my wife's friends. Josh and I hung out at the Oasis Saloon when our wives took yoga class together. Then one day Josh called up and said he was going cold turkey: no more beer, no more drinking at all. We could still be friends and I could even drink in front of him, but we couldn't go to bars. I was game at first, meeting him at sushi places as he seemed to have replaced hops and barley for fish and rice. I drank sake and contributed my end of the small talk until the glow of rice wine spread to my cheeks.

Once we had locked the doors of the Oasis Saloon from the inside when Natasha the bartender had gone out for a smoke. Josh and I were the only ones there that afternoon besides an old rummy named Sven who was such a constant presence Natasha joked that the owner claimed him as a dependent. While Natasha banged on the door and hollered that she'd kick our asses, Josh and I poured ourselves pints and got pretzels for Sven who took them without comment as if he thought we worked there. I flung wet napkins at the pressed tin ceiling, which is pretty juvenile, but it's a lot of pressure to be clever in the spur of the moment, although not for Josh: locking the door on Natasha had been his idea. When we did let her back in, she was pretty pissed but couldn't make a big deal because if Tony found out she left the register unattended she'd be in bigger trouble. Tony was fine with me. He always slid me a beer on the house when the Ice Hogs won. He also owned the Gyro stand across the street and the regulars were allowed to order from the carry-out menu taped to the register. Tony would send over one of the fry guys with a bag of food and ketchup packets.

WHEN MY COUSIN DREW started to pick up the pieces of his life, he invited me out for coffee so he could officially make amends. "I'm sorry about creating distances between you and other people," Drew told me earnestly. Too earnestly for my taste but he seemed confident, like he knew what he was doing. The waitress at Perkins switched out our carafe, which we had already gotten down to a quarter full. She had lots of eye liner and let her hip stick out when she poured. I fell in love with every girl who ever waited on me.

I told Drew, "I don't feel like you created a distance between me and anyone."

He stirred cream into his coffee and lots of sugar, a new packet after every sip almost. He said, "By telling you about the other women I forced you away from my wife."

What was I supposed to say? That I forgave him? Or was he supposed to have to work for it? I genuinely didn't know since Josh had quit without meetings or amends. At least he never made any to me. I liked hearing Drew's druggie stories and a little distance between me and other people seemed a reasonable price. Drew and Josh were sober now, closer to their wives but farther from me. In the end it just came down to physics.

"Am I an alcoholic?" I asked. It was at that moment I got his attention, a new story.

"I don't know," he said. "It isn't for me to decide. But it is a question alcoholics ask. So that's useful data, right? That you're asking yourself that."

"I'm not asking myself. I'm asking you."

"Grandpa Henry was a drunk," Drew said. "Our dads act like they do because they were raised with a lot of yelling and hitting. It's why they were both so volatile."

"Volatile," I repeated, mostly just to hear it come out of my mouth.

"If you're worried about it, come to a meeting with me. You can just sit and listen. In the meantime, don't have a beer tonight. Then see if you can go without one tomorrow."

I considered it, but stopped at the bar on my way home anyway. My calculation was that I could skip the beer just to make a point, just to show myself a story about going a day without a drink. On the other hand, just walking into the Oasis Saloon made me feel better. Even if you don't have a buddy to go with, you still feel like a king sidling up to the bar, giving a nod to Sven, Natasha already pouring your beer before you ask. If that doesn't make you feel like royalty, you can even get a gyro with onion rings delivered right to you, you don't even have to get off the stool. I would be very surprised if sobriety felt much better than that.

Half a Song

He was most aware of his buttery smell here at his son's piano lessons: French fry oil from his short sleeve shirt, khaki pants spotted from cheddar biscuits, all oppressively pungent here in Ms. Walters' sweetly appointed piano studio. Ms. Walters had a potpourri bowl that she had begun putting out for Nelson's lessons and Henry was pretty sure it was because of how he smelled—and not just the food but sweat and hair grease too. He originally hoped Ms. Walters would take an interest in him, a working class guy making an effort to better his son through music lessons, a divorced dad with sole custody of the child: that in itself should be interesting enough to spark a couple of conversations. Ms. Walters— with her long curly hair and floral shirts—was the only real female authority figure Nelson had, at least in the summer. Somehow, no matter how much joking around he did before and after lessons, no matter how familiar he behaved toward Ms. Walters, no matter how much she seemed to like Nelson or how many recitals he had taken Nelson to so they could watch Ms. Walters play Beethoven sonatas or duets with other musicians, nothing came of it.

"Nelson's sight reading of this piece has really improved," Ms. Walters would say things like that over her shoulder as the boy stood and gathered his sheet music. Though she started each lesson on her stool, she usually ended up on the piano bench next to Nelson, placing his hands on the correct keys or grabbing his hands to curl his fingers for the same reason a master gardener might get frustrated watching an amateur till soil. "I can tell he worked hard this week."

"The swimming coach will be mad tomorrow." Henry rose from the padded armchair where he observed from across the small studio. "But irregardless, we wanted him to get the fingering on *Claire de la Lune* right."

Nelson glowered and would complain later that the swimming comment had been "embarrassing." Henry had never been able to get past this sort of chit-chat with Ms. Walters.

Toward the end of Nelson's first year of piano lessons, when Ms. Walters announced her engagement and then married a cellist from the Greater Rockford Area Symphonic Orchestra, Henry had immediately wanted to stop going to lessons, even thought about canceling his last check with the bank so Ms. Walters couldn't cash it, but that seemed too obvious. It would be clear that Nelson had been coming because of her. On inertia alone he had continued to work a split shift at Mister Sea Food so he could get home, bring Nelson to the lesson where Henry occasionally fell asleep. After the lesson, Henry would take Nelson home and get back to the restaurant just at the start of the dinner rush when the tips were slightly better.

"Did you remember to practice the glissandos, Nelson? No? Like this."

The kid wasn't getting any better—he might actually be getting *worse*—but Henry couldn't figure a way to stop the lessons. Ms. Walters leaned across the boy and threw her arms over his, brushed the keys back and forth. The kid had begun looking down her shirt during these moments, Henry could tell.

Just before she got married, Ms. Walters gave them an invitation. She hadn't mailed it, just handed it to Nelson to "give to your dad." Henry dutifully dressed himself and

Nelson for the event, even negotiated with Janice for a different visiting weekend so they could go. Only, it turned out they hadn't been invited to the wedding, just a reception for all of her piano students and his cello kids. Henry walked around with a small glass of punch and looked into the eyes of the other fathers to see if any of them were just as dead. He put an envelope with a check on the table though he was sure the card was too fancy and the amount too high.

"Do you wanna quit?" he had asked Nelson any number of times after the marriage. The boy hated practicing but would only shrug his shoulders when Henry offered to end it.

"Maybe when summer starts," Nelson would mutter to his shoes.

During that first year of marriage to the cellist, Henry watched Mrs. Tsumisato—her new name—go through a number of changes. She got larger, not fat, just heavier in spirit; her face became splotchy and ashen. He expected an announcement of a child but it never came. Then she cut her hair short and told Henry she was going to be taking a few months off for health reasons.

"Is everything okay?" Henry asked.

"Oh fine," she said smiling. "Not to worry."

He struggled for something to say, something buoying. "We all have our trials I guess," he said, shrugging.

He didn't exactly believe it, but she had nodded, maybe even gotten a little misty.

"That's true, Mr. Metzler," Mrs. Tsumisato said. "We must face our troubles with all the dignity the Lord has given."

Henry nodded soberly and thought about dignity. That very day, just before the lesson, a family had come into the restaurant with a child having a second birthday and Henry had to sing the Mister Sea Food Birthday song by himself because all other waiters were busy. His voice had cracked on the line "*And the fishy fishy fishies love you-oooo,*" it would have been embarrassing if he'd had any dignity left.

When Ms. Walters returned from hiatus, (he couldn't bring himself to use the cello teacher's name), Henry searched her face for clues as to what happened. Her complexion seemed to have cleared and her hair was still short but growing back and she seemed beautiful to him again. He realized it was more than interest he had in Ms. Walters, he was actually in love with her, and that it was going to be an unrequited sort of love, which really is the worst, the stupidest kind of love there is. Janice had stopped saying she loved him once they married, and even then she had only said it when she was kidding, being grand and old fashioned to point out how square he was in comparison to her. Janice was currently living with a man and a woman—a couple—and Henry was unsure of the exact nature of the relationship, though he felt shooting pains in his stomach when he thought about his son's weekend visits.

Henry watched the piano teacher's exaggerated swaying as she worked a section of *Arietta* with Nelson, and Henry's desire for a romance with this woman became a real presence in the room. The affair he envisioned would be old-fashioned, classical, like the stately busts of the composers around the studio. He imagined them in European drawing rooms listening to private arias and riding in sleeper cars and listening to the radio for news broadcasts. He had talked to the cellist at the wedding and a few other times as well and Henry found him to be nerdy and self-involved, a nervous person. He was probably a good cellist, Henry couldn't tell, but that had to be the only explanation why someone like Ms. Walters would—could—be attracted to someone like that.

At home, just when Nelson wasn't around, Henry plinked on the piano himself. If he tried hard he could work out a melody with a single finger, make it sound like half a song if he worked at it. Henry soon found himself making up a melody. With one finger he would tap it out and when he found a wrong note, he would hum it out loud as if he could explain to the piano what he wanted to hear. *Bum bum bum. . . .* What he was playing was familiar, but new at the same time: a song for Ms. Walters. He could play it with one finger, three notes here, jump a few keys over, play two more, hit a black key then down, then another black key. It gave Henry the same feeling he had when the doctor first put a scope to Janice's belly and he heard the first whoosh of Nelson's blood: the start of something magical.

The day Nelson came home from school early because he threw up in gym, Henry was given permission to leave Mister Sea Food in the middle of lunch and pick him up. Henry set the child up with the TV and box of crackers. He told him, "I'm going to the piano lesson for you." The boy seemed confused by this, but Henry went to the piano and played his short melody one more time.

He sat in the piano studio and listened to a new student play *Twinkle Twinkle* and remembered fondly Nelson's early struggles. Henry suddenly felt awash in a warm gratitude toward Ms. Walters. He forgave Ms. Walters for marrying the cello player and tapped his song on the armrest of the padded chair.

When the new boy finished and his mother removed him, Ms. Walters smiled at Henry the way one does at a familiar and comforting face. "Is Nelson in the washroom?"

"No, Mrs. Tsumisato. He's sick. But I came anyway because I wanted to show you something. May I sit?" He indicated the piano bench and she nodded cautiously. He stuffed himself between the bench and the piano feeling nervous, overwhelmed.

"Are you going to play something, Mr. Metzler? I didn't know you played piano."

"I'd like to, yes. But I've never played anything on the piano before, so. Forgive me." He wasn't sure what he was saying.

"You need to pull the bench out a little," she told him.

He stood and let her reposition the bench and remove the boxes the smaller children used to rest their feet. Henry turned to his left and smiled. Ms. Walters took her position on her stool and looked at him with some curiosity.

"Well," he said at last. "I have a song."

"A song?"

"Really a melody only." He felt brave using the correct term: melody. "Just a little something I've been hearing in my head. And I was wondering if you could help me by filling in the other parts, make it a whole song."

"A whole. . . ."

"Well, that we could work it out together." He found a groove now in talking. "That I could play the melody and then together, me and you, together we could work out the whole song that would go around the melody. I can only play it with one finger, but if you could show me, with both hands, how someone takes a melody and adds the bottom hand—"

"Chords?"

"Yes, chords. And then how you move the top hand around so it isn't just the single note."

"It's been a while since I tried to arrange a piece of music. But let me hear your song."

He was surprised to see his hand shaking when he touched the piano. He thought to apologize but she was smiling so warmly at him that he was able to continue.

He hit the first few notes and stopped. "That was too fast," he told her.

"Go ahead," she said sweetly. "Try again."

He played the notes again, slower, the whole thing was only ten seconds long really, maybe twenty notes, and he tried again. She nodded as he played, looked off into the distance. Ms. Walters was listening.

"*Bum bum bum*," she said quietly. "Oh, I think I got this. Play it again."

He began the song a third time, and now it sounded exactly right to him, dignified yet whimsical, an expression of what life could be like for the two of them.

She began smiling. "Got it," she said. From the stool, she leaned and put her hands on the keys and began playing.

"Yes," Henry said right away. She had chords in the left hand and something busier in the right, but it was still his melody he could hear. It was as he imagined it. It was as though she had been able to look into his heart and play it *exactly* as he heard it.

And then she started singing words as she went, "Tasty and good...." she sang. And then, "Always the freshest catch in the sea...."

Henry felt the blood rush from his face.

"Is that right?" she asked. "The Mister Sea Food song? Isn't that where you work?" She started playing it from the beginning again. "*Where you wanna go when the fun gotta be good, and the fish gotta be fresh, and the chum gotta hum....*"

Henry's throat was dry. "I wanted to learn the jingle. To surprise my boss."

"Oh, sure," she said sweetly. "Of course, I already know it. It's amazing how something ridiculous can take up so much room in our heads. But I can teach you simple technique Mr. Metzler, teach you how to play your song. It'll be nice working with an adult for a change!"

And she came off the stool and put herself right next to Henry on the bench, arranging herself so they were hip to hip. Henry took a breath as Mrs. Tsumisato put her hands on the keys and began teaching him to play.

The Fat Man's Corpse

It was her idea to get the body of the fat man and live inside of it. It didn't have to be a fat man, a large man would do, but someone big enough to fit both.

"You can work the left side, and I'll work the right," she told him. He watched her slice down the center, top of the skull to the tip of the penis, and scoop out the insides like a pumpkin.

"Help me with this," she told him. "When I fill this bucket, you dump it into the sewer and then bring it back to me."

Finally she had cleared enough room for them both to crawl inside, and she zipped them up, as if the fat man were a sleeping bag. He put both his legs and feet into the fat man's left leg, and she did the same with the right. They leaned on each other for support, arms wrapped around each other's shoulders where the rib cage had been. Then she sewed the body back up from the inside so that they were securely within.

The wife swung her leg and the husband tipped forward and swung his leg. It was fun to walk like that. The fat man looked like a military man marching while drunk. The husband's and wife's cheeks rubbed against each other, inside the head of the fat man. Her blue eye was in one socket and his brown eye was in the other. They looked in the mirror and waved.

"Hi honey," the husband said, and the fat man waved with his left arm.

Then she waved and said, "Hi honey. Hi right back at you."

At night they leaned back and the fat man toppled into their bed. They both laughed and moved around. The husband turned to face the wife and put both his legs backwards into the fat man's. The husband rutted on top of his wife hard. His rearend slapped against the lining of the fat man's stomach, but the wife took her arms and held on to the husband so he couldn't move up and down so far. The husband liked that, and howled deeply.

"Fantastic," he told her. "Did you come?"

"No," she said. "But I enjoyed it and I'm glad you came."

"Should we get out of the fat man?" he asked.

"I like this just fine," she told him. "Let's stay inside."

In the morning they took their regular walking positions and went to the kitchen. The wife took a pot out of the cupboard and the husband used his arm to take off the lid.

"Put the lid on the counter," she said to him. "And then you can turn on the faucet." The wife was already holding the pot under the tap, and it filled with water. "Now we're going to boil eggs. I hope you like eggs."

"You know I do," the husband said.

"Now where did I put the salt?"

The husband bristled. "If you could get yourself organized a little better—"

"Shhh. . ." She didn't feel like hearing that same old speech again, not when they were on the verge of something new. He took the shushing without complaint although it irked him even more than her laissez-faire attitude towards housework.

They walked around the town, always bending down to look at their face reflected in public fountains or in polished hubcaps. They walked into clothing stores and paused at the three-way mirrors or the display cases that reflected their oneness back at them.

The wife had always felt a tension in their marriage. It had always been her pulling close and her husband pulling away, her talking silly talk and her husband putting an end to it, her spilling something and her husband yelling after her. To relieve themselves of the tension they fucked each other, they threw plates, they called each other names. *Idiot* they said, *putain*! They had used all the words in the book.

Now there was no tension. They went for walks. They got a dog and fed him. Sometimes they read a book in the evening or looked at TV. The programs weren't funny, but they laughed because they wanted to. All the songs on the radio sounded good now. They danced inside the fat man, even to the songs they used to hate. She was very pleased with the new arrangement, although occasionally she would rub her hand against the fat man's belly and wonder if it would be possible—if they both worked really hard—to reduce the fat man's paunch or maybe tone up some of the flabby skin in the arms and legs. She never said anything about it to her husband because she thought it would make her seem shallow.

In a junk shop she found two blue marbles. She put one up against her eye and another against his. She asked, "Wouldn't these make marvelous eyes for us? No one would ever be able to tell that we are a we."

He considered the cost. Since they had put on this second skin they had saved quite a bit of money. They hadn't gone out to eat or to the movies and he had just written a check to a credit card company for more than the minimum payment. A zero balance was an elusive shoreline and the husband fantasized about making that final payment. It was her spending that had gotten them in debt, he told himself. She was too blasé about all matters pecuniary. This bothered him even more than being shooshed. But he agreed to buy the marbles because they had been getting along and he didn't want to ruin it with a fight. He took out the wallet which he kept on his side of the fat man. He could mention the spending later if he had to.

With the new blue eyes in place, they were completely safe inside the fat man. Nobody ever suspected them. Together the fat man moved to a new town and got a job and joined a church. He made a friend or two.

In public he spoke in the husband's voice, but the wife was in on all the decisions. He wrote checks to the utilities and the credit card companies using his new fat man signature, and never mentioned his concerns about spending. Eventually she stopped worrying about the way the fat man looked and decided that it was what was inside a person that counted.

Sometimes they talked with each other, deep within the countenance of the fat man, but when they talked they seemed to say the same thing, often at the same time, until at last they did not bother anymore. They were the fat man, an inflatable boat floating on a motionless sea. They were the fat man sitting quietly or reading the paper or deciding to fix himself popcorn in the evenings. All by himself like this he began to wish for things. He invented memories of women who had been interested in him. He imagined himself a family. At night he rocked in his rocking chair, wishing for a companion.

a paire of new & Artificial eyes

Jews of old Amsterdam step off dry canvas—they have been shaped quickly but are still recognizable, smeared and rubbed and scratched with blunt tipped brushes—paint splotches flung from a distance from the imprecise fingers of their creator. In twos and threes they walk the dry corridors of the Met where they take tea in the Wright house and eat sliced pound cake, leaving behind crumpled balls of cellophane for the cleaning staff. The children play tag in the glass-roofed gardens and touch the *tchotchke* in the gift shop, clicking the tops of pens and scribbling on sample pads. Mothers journey to the cafeteria and poke at the flaky meat sandwiches wrapped in foil, they daub giant tubs of sauces and lick thick orange and yellow goop from their own imprecise fingers. They bring back clear plastic boxes of assorted vegetables to their families. The men and women talk good-naturedly about their dress; they have been adorned in clothing from the Bible and in Renaissance robes instead of the scarves and dark hats of their own golden age.

Baruch Spinoza the Lens Maker is among them, here, walking the halls with his fellow ex-countrymen. The Jews are not afraid to approach him despite rabbinical decree forbidding it. What would be the point of maintaining such malevolence *here*? They wave and call his name, Bento or Baruch or even Benjamin, Benny, or Benji-boy. *How's bid-ness,* a Burgher calls to him. Spinoza shrugs his shoulders. "A grind," he answers grinning, palms open. Wordplay and comic gestures have replaced prayer as spiritual currency of the day. Spinoza is well suited for this day, though he knows not what day it is or on what map he might locate this new Amsterdam.

REMBRANDT VAN RIJN LOVES the streets of old Amsterdam, the only city on Earth whose denizens share his passion for sartorial flourish and who understand his near pathological need to dress up. The Dutch dress the way he paints, tinkering and fussing over each detail: the angle of a feather in a hat, the direction lace falls across a shoulder. Layering is what resonates so deeply with the master, the long dark *huiks,* the wonderful conical hats that require a stick to keep erect, the severe sleeves sewn to the bodices. A woman might have one or two or three petticoats of contrasting colors peeking out at the edges of her dress as she makes her way down the market stalls, fingering the sugar herrings. As the master negotiates his way through a basket of cheese or butter, he might be struck dumb by the shades in a single scarf. The idea that any one of these well coifed women on the street might be peeled like a magical plum with endless skins, each layer hiding the nectar a bit lower, makes even the most mundane errand drag on for hours. His wife Cornelia knows to never expect Remmy to take less than an afternoon on an errand as simple as purchasing the night's dinner cake.

In his studio he dresses the subjects of his paintings not for historical function—he might group peasant gowns of the Renaissance in the same frame as papal finery—but because he can't stop adding layers. Posing for the master has a reputation as a being pretty tedious way to earn a florin. If one sits twelve hours for a portrait, seven of them are spent with the master fussing over the way a millstone hangs from your neck or the repose of a single feather on a debutante. *Leave it for chrissakes,* a model will exasperatedly slap his hand as he endlessly places and re-places brooch or bracelet. *Just paint it how you want, but leave me alone already.* Rembrandt would laugh, look to the mirrors on the ceiling, glance at the arched reflectors behind the subject, the heavy prism refracting color from the ceiling, the pulsing light ball from the box in the corner, arrange his mirror tubes, moisten his brush, then decide suddenly a coat had been laced incorrectly or a shoe had been polished too much and now required scuffing.

Because Rembrandt was one of the few gentiles allowed to live in the Jewish quarter, he was often summoned on official business to meet with the Calvinist overseers. Usually there was a pretext, a rent dispute or an underpayment from one of the guilds, but Rembrandt knew the real purpose was to size him up to be sure he hadn't gone *shtetel.* Remmy hated these interruptions to his routine, filled with reassurances and double-talk, *No he hadn't stepped foot in the synagogue. No, he never allowed a Jew in his home after dark. Yes, he crossed the canal on Sundays for church.*

There are new concerns, Van Rijn, the overlord Jann Van Der Meer told him sternly. There was always a new concern. The Calvinists were always in a snit about something. The Calvinists were mad because St. Luke was out and Minerva was in. Morals were slipping. They worried about war with the French. They worried that beards were disappearing, and worse, hair on women was getting so long one couldn't tell a Dutch woman from an Italian.

Van Der Meer shrugged his shoulders. *We are seeing too much of you in your paintings, not enough glory unto He who gives you talent.*

It had been coming for some time. More than anything he loved to paint himself, taking great pride in arranging his mirrors and devices to emphasize fatty tissues and bruises and the droopy skin hanging under his eyes. It wasn't his reflection that inspired him, that dross and flabby bag of bones he carried around, but something about the mirror, something about the reflection itself, the wrestling of that reflection onto a canvas. It was while looking into the lenses of his light-box reflector that he had seen for the first time the hopeless unevenness of his face. Up until then he had been certain that both halves of his face were identical, mirror images of themselves, and once he had seen this unevenness in his own face, he could detect it in others with his naked eye. The people around him were similarly misshapen, imperfect.

We need to see a deeper reflection of your gratitude onto the Lord Van Der Meer scolded Rembrandt. *We need to see your appreciation of your special status with The Guild.*

I understand, Remmy told him. I understand.

BARUCH SPINOZA'S GRANDFATHER had come from Portugal with nothing: empty pockets and old clothing on his back. His only possession was the seventy-three names of the Almighty, the contours of which were in-scripted on his heart, and he often muttered them, alphabetically, to himself while fishing in the Amstel or clomping along the Houtgracht where he lived. "Aleph, Adloose, Beholder...." Now Bento had a home. He and his family were members of several professional guilds and he could walk around the canvases of the Great Master Rembrandt and inspect the work. He was twelve, and three months shy of his bar mitzvah. He took the canvases in quickly, rushing past like the wheel-carted fruit vendors, glossing the faces and colors in the tableaus, at once stopping so abruptly that he raised his arms to keep from teetering forward. From across the studio Rembrandt could see the boy's face color, the shame working its way from shoulders to contorted brow. Bento paused before a medium-sized canvas. In a swirl of colors and motions it depicted a woman, large nose and world-weary face, thick arms like a man, being robustly fucked by a bearded man in red biblical robes. The woman's legs wrapped around her congressional-interlocutor's middle, one hand gripping his neck and the other the man's hip, as though to keep from being thrown. He suckled the woman's teats through her robe. Bento had never seen anything quite so obscene.

"That's just Jacob Wrestling with the Angel," Rembrandt called.

Bento recognized in the face of the angel, her face sober, focused only on coming, that of a woman on his block, Rachel, one of the few enjoined Hebrews. By fiat of the congressional council none were allowed to speak to Rachel on the Sabbath and she herself was forbidden to enter Synagogue. Rachel's face was so real, so gloriously rippling with emergent pleasure, so clearly struggling even to contain that pleasure, that he almost looked away from shame.

"They'll never buy it," Bento finally murmured when the master had come and placed a steady hand on his shoulder.

Rembrandt chuckled, "I've already sold it, smart guy." He gave the boy a little nudge, breaking the gaze. "A Calvinist will buy whatever a merchant has to sell." He looked at the painting again, trying to see it from the boy's point of view. "I guess I could put wings on her," he said at last.

THAT AFTERNOON FORWARD Bento feared seeing Rachel on the street, knowing what he knew—not just that it was possible to look into a woman's eyes while committing an adulterous act, but that it was probably true the master harbored such intimate knowledge through his own experience. He spent more time in the master's studio now, posing as Isaac for a depiction of Abraham sacrificing his son. Each time he feared seeing Rachel playing cards with the master's wife, or seeing her pouring lighting oil into a copper lamp.

Rembrandt removed Bento's shirt and studied his hairless chest and pasty white limbs. He lay Bento down on a reclining chair and arranged a towel around Bento's waist. It had to be just right, and the master tied one end around the other, covering Bento's groin and pulling the fabric below his navel, just to the top of his pubes. He made the boy hold his arms behind him and when that didn't look real enough, he cut the tassels from an old rug of his landlords and bound Bento's arms tightly behind him. Bento complained, but his arms looked pained and wearied, the veins stuck out and his shoulders rounded off nicely. Rembrandt pushed his head back and when his meaty palm nearly covered Bento's delicate face, he looked at his own hand and he realized something about the scene. He had planned to have Isaac's eyes open with the loving trust a son gives to a father, but with Bento's face now covered by his own hand, with his chin the only visible adornment between his thumb and forefinger, he realized something about a father's love for a son. Abraham would not want Isaac to see the blade as he stuck it into his white body, he would try to shield his son from his own betrayal. Rembrandt placed his mirror and his hand back over Bento and saw that this was how he would paint the scene. He held the knife just over Bento's flat arched body, the gleaming blade long and still with a slight curve near the tip, he took a few practiced swings as if getting ready to really insert in the body.

"You aren't really going to cut me, are you?" Bento tried to joke but could hear the doubt in his own voice.

"Shhhh. . ."

"Because you do know what the story is, right? There isn't any need to see what I would look like with blood coming from my flesh."

Rembrandt had planned to have the angel appearing over Isaac's prone body, arms flailing and eyes wide—don't do it, the face would read—but he decided now it would be more dramatic to have the angel's hand on Abraham's arm, gripping Abraham's wrist and the knife just slipping from his grasp, and Abraham looking startled as if he was just getting ready to rip when the Angel appeared.

While Rembrandt painted Spinoza, he talked to him.

"You know, a lot of the stuff I read in that book," Rembrandt indicated with a paint specked thumb the open German tome behind him. "A lot of it doesn't square with what I know about life."

"Those are called miracles," Spinoza told him.

"That's right," Rembrandt nodded as if remembering at last. "Miracles. A sea opens up." He looked over his shoulder conspiratorially, "The moribund heart of a corpse beats again. Miracles. Still. It's funny. God, you know, so unknowable and all. Infinite. You can't even comprehend the infiniteness of not knowing how infinite he is. Yes?"

Spinoza ran the words over in his mind and knew them to be meaningless. The Master was pretending to be pretending, acting like an actor who acts in the play, the part of an actor in the second play, buried inside the first play. "But look at that," he pointed archly toward the Bible again. "There's a whole book about He who can't be written about. And look at this." He swiveled an easel at Spinoza to show the boy a half sketched, half colored canvas; there was the sea and above that clouds, and above that God in all his robes and fires and ghostly appearing from the heavens gesturing at two figures leaving the garden.

"Who's this?" Rembrandt asked.

"God."

"Right. I've painted God. He's unseeable but I painted him. Didn't take especially long either, some yellow, white for the beard, soaking the chalk for that soft-affect, that's what took the most time. Still, didn't even have to draw the whole body which is kind of a bonus. Like drawing a leper. Just kind of have it blending into the sky here and what have you. Yet you recognized him anyway."

Now he licked his lips and brought forth a round orb just under Spinoza's face. "The Calvinists are looking in the wrong places, that's what makes a Calvinist a Calvinist. They look up. Let Galileo look up at dots in the sky. You know what he finds? More dots, more abstraction. Anton van Leeuwenhoek, you know the name? You will. He's invented a telescope for looking inward, for looking down." He held his arm aloft, stroking the thick hair under Bento's eyes. "Van Leeunhoek finds more life on his arm than in all the heavens your scopes can reach. On our hair, life. He's seen the infinitesimal, the insensible, impalpable, indiscernible, the heretofore evanescent parts of our life."

Baruch caught sight of himself in the mirror then and looked at his adolescent face, acne and little childish teen-aged moustache. He peered closer at the hairs, he looked a moment at the pimples dotting the topography of his face, and then he looked away.

IN THE EVENING Bento thought about it:

And the more he posed for the master, the more he saw himself not a part of the glory of God's creations as had been billed in the work-flyer, but in just the reflected glory on Rembrandt's easel. Evenings found him sullen and disquieted, and he pushed aside herring and drank only hot tea, letting a lump of hardened sugar dissolve between his teeth. He held a slice of pickled egg once, staring into the segment, thinking what it might look like under one of the Master's lenses micro-telescopes. Even with cheap tallow and his own sharp eyes he could discern roughness in the green yolk where he had heretofore assumed smoothness; a universe of tactility upon the entire ovum where Bento had not even been aware enough to be aware of all he might not be aware of. This discovery so mesmerized the boy he was surprised to find as he crawled into bed many hours later that he still clutched the sodden yolk.

"Aleph, Adloose, Beholder, Belover, Benzoor. . . ."

Manasseh Ben Israel himself had come to synagogue one Yom Kippur extolling the wonders of what he had seen looking into a German telescope. "If we look into the heavens itself then who knows, perhaps we can expand the known names of He Who Keeps Tabs on Us tenfold. Imagine knowing 100 names of God, or 1,000, or. . ." and he had been too overcome to finish this particular thought, the hunched men davening and murmuring to quell this vision. Bento licked his lips. Someday there might be so many names of the Lord that it would literally take a lifetime to say them all.

"Not 100 names of the Almighty," he said out loud to his egg. "But fifty. Or ten." It struck him like a bright yellow thunderclap of a painting, of art, that looking inward he should try to decrease the number of words for God, maybe get it down to just two or even one. Or even less than that.

IT WOULD BE WEEKS BEFORE Bento would catch a glimpse of Rachel out on the street, arguing with a monger with all the emotion she could muster from her withered, hungry frame. *This is your blood,* she shouted, fingering an eel with a rough finger. "Fresh, fresh," came the thickly accented protest, for who else would haggle with such a woman? *This fish is as old as I am. You spilled your blood on it to make it look fresh. . . .*

Rachelle and the vendor huddled closer to the wax papered eel, each looking for evidence of the other's claim, looking closer. Where was God? God was above and God was below and God was everywhere. God was in the fish and in the blood of the vendor on the fish and Rachel's determined face, the lines of concentration on the master's tablet bringing forth an orgasm. Bento looked away.

He must avoid that face, the image of that pleasure, Bento looked down, looked deep at the cobblestone glinting under the afternoon sun. A puddle, or "poodle" as his German landlord would say, had formed in the indentations of the carved stone. Bento had begun carving lenses now, had begun putting them together too and he was now able to see things deeper, smaller than even the Master had imagined possible —whole societies in soup, a quivering universe inside a cup of flan. But now on the street he saw his own reflection oddly, as a series of fragmented lines—something he had surely seen before and yet, spinning, he had seen deeper and deeper into the shadows and shapes of his fragmented reflection, and as he knelt down to gaze deeper, a pebble kicked from a running goyim child splattered the puddle and the reflection was suddenly scattered, leaving only stone.

I Am the Light

My name is Howard. I am the light.

At first I was unaware of this, as you are now. But like you I came to understand what I am and what I must do.

I am the way.

Everything I do becomes legend. Remember the rock group Big Panty? Remember their slogan: DO BONGS?

I used to work for them. I knew them in high school before they were making any money. I used to move all their equipment around from one show to another. A show in those days was somebody's basement and a party. It was fun.

They were the band but I was the man. They even said so. Between numbers I would call, "Do bongs, Do bongs" and soon everyone was shouting it.

Even now that they are big and play the big halls people are still yelling "Do bongs." They yell it from the streets when the Big Panty party limo drives by. They chant it on television shows when Big Panty is on. I am no longer with Big Panty but "Do bongs" lives on and on.

There's a little rock trivia for you. They used to laugh when someone would say "Do bongs." They aren't laughing now of course. Now they hear cash registers.

It is legend just as I too am legend. I am Howard. I am the light.

I WENT TO MR. DONUTS once and saw a girl whose entire face was covered with burns; but her hair was beautiful. It was a brilliant fiery red. It seemed likely that her hair was what had set fire to her face.

I THOUGHT ABOUT STRIKING up a conversation but it was very late and the only people about were lost spirits and perverts. I didn't want to frighten her.

Besides, I could see her reflection in the mirror eating a donut. She had no upper lip and her top row of teeth was encrusted with yellow muck. She could not keep the donut from spilling out of her mouth. She used one hand to hold the donut and the other to retrieve the pieces that fell, and then stuffed them back under her yellow teeth.

I admired her greatly and wanted to talk to her. But it was late and though I am not a lost soul or a pervert, I could not think of a way to begin talking to her.

And when the loneliness washes over me, I have to remember; unlike you, I am here for a reason. I cannot see a movie every time I don't want to think. I cannot pick up a phone each time the sounds of my own thoughts are insufficient. I cannot bowl instead of cry. It is important to know that to be the one, as I am, I must be ONE.

The reason the music is so loud is so I can hear it. I have to hear it. I have to be able to hear it. Long shot, liquidator. Nobody is special.

I TELL YOU THIS NOT by way of explanation. I tell you this not so you can nod your head and say, "See?" But I do want you to know that I spent some time locked away.

I had a lot of books all neatly packed away on shelves. When they found me, all my books were heaped into the center of my room. I was sleeping on top of the pile.

THE PROBLEM WAS THAT I hadn't answered the phone in several weeks. The problem was I ignored the doorbell. I didn't eat. I didn't hallucinate like they said I would.

I participated in osmosis.

And when they came in and found me and yanked me off my support systems, I didn't fight. I let my Walkman drop to the ground. My body rose, lifted upwards. I saw it all before my door actually came down for the benefit of the less divine. It was all there: hoses, screaming, the smell of charcoal. I can't explain it except to say that it happened.

"DO BONGS," I TOLD the fireman. He nodded, wrapped me in a sheet, ate a donut. Me too.

I HAVE A PLAID BAG that I keep my bowling ball in. I found the bowling ball in a gutter. It was in the plaid bag. I keep the ball and the bag together because that's the way I found them.

The Irish have a similar thing for their tea pots. They call them Tea Cozies. An Irish girl named Christine told me about it one night.

She was a fan of the band I used to work for, Big Panty. I used to see her at all the shows. She had amazing red hair that used to fight the light for brilliance. I actually once had a conversation with her. I couldn't keep my eyes off her hair. We talked about tea cozies.

"You actually put them over your tea kettles?" I asked.

"Mm-hmmm," she laughed. "We knit them."

AND THIS IS HOW I GET to sleep at night: I lay in bed on the covers and close my eyes. Then I pretend I'm being shot in the head. I flinch and convulse three times as three bullets enter my skull and blood showers my face.

Then I attempt to crawl out, but I am losing strength so fast I can only make it to the edge of the bed. I reach up for the phone but I can only raise my arm a little off the sheets before I collapse altogether in a heap. Then I sleep.

BUT I AM ALWAYS ABLE to fill with blood and rise up. I am the erection. Through me you will find love and joy and an ocean of harmony. I have seen the after-world. It is as written, and St. Peter will greet each and everyone of you. "Do bongs," he will say. "Do bongs St. Peter," you will say back to him. He'll grin and let you pass.

I am that merry wise man.

THE REASON I CAN SEE the girl so well in the window is because I have no lips either. I have been through it, boy! I have walked through fire and lived.

But now you wouldn't know me from Adam.

The fire fighters think that they extinguished the blaze. They didn't. They carried it out on a stretcher and brought it home. They gave it oxygen. They fanned the flames and sent it out on its way.

You can see the flames licking my face. You can only look for a second before it gets too bright and hurts your eyes. Look away. Don't point, child. Don't stare.

There but for the grace of me go you.

IT ALSO WORKS for television too.

When the show stops I get sad. And the commercials take so long. Sometimes I can't barely take it no more. I lay back in the chair and pretend bullets are pelting my body. I shake and quiver and flail about, but there is no escape. They eventually stop, but it is too late.

THE BLOOD IS DRAINING from me but still I want to raise my arms to my Father and beg forgiveness. I can't get them up and soon I lose consciousness.

Then the show comes back on.

MY HAIR WAS NOT TOUCHED by the flames. I don't exactly know why, but it is the truth. My entire body was consumed with fire like the burning bush. But I did not speak. I had long red hair, and I still do. I have lost everything but the red hair. It is all gone except for my hair.

The Mr. Donut is the only thing open late at night and that is why I go there. The guy behind the counter is huge. Flesh bursts out of him on all sides. He nods to me and does not stare at my dry face. He doesn't seem to mind that I have no upper lip. This isn't easy to say, but he never, he never says anything. He never looks away. He never flinches. He gives me my cruller and my coffee and I pay him and I leave. It is the only thing I really look forward to during the day. I look forward to the day becoming night so I can get a donut.

I LIKE THE FAT GUY that works behind the counter at Mr. Donut. He talks to me and doesn't flinch. He asks if I've found work yet. I shake my head no. He tells me it's tough. He puts sugar and milk in my coffee. I don't have to ask any more. When he takes my money I can taste powdered sugar. He seems to exhale it. When he brings me my change he nods and tells me to have a good night.

I nod. I sit in the booth and turn on my Walkman loud. Maybe I listen to Fuzzbox or the Go-Go's or maybe today I want to hear Sinéad. I open the best seller I brought with me and read. I can eat with one hand and catch all the food that comes rolling past my charred lips with the other.

SOMETIMES PEOPLE COME IN and get donuts and sometimes they actually stay. Nobody sits in the booths near me. No one talks to me. I couldn't hear them if they did. The music fills my head. It is good. I never listen to Big Panty.

Once a girl came in that I recognized. I think she used to come see the band I worked for. They were good once. You may have heard of them. Big Panty.

I used to see this girl at the shows before the fire. Before she got burned up real bad. She had this amazing red hair that I could see from backstage. It would swirl around her head as she danced like a moving halo. When I came up to her she would talk to me because I wore a Big Panty All Access necklace. She knew I could get her backstage. And I did one night. It may even have been the night of the fire. It may not have been. I don't remember.

At the Mr. Donut she didn't even look my way. She wouldn't have recognized me if she did, but I might have at least reminded her of something. She's gone now and I never said anything to her. She probably thinks I was killed in the fire like so many others do.

You would be surprised at how many people think that. They don't know that I am the fire. I became the fire. Just as Mr. Donut is powdered sugar, I am the fire and the light and the way and the truth. I am.

DR. ROY EUCLID TOLD ME that it might be easier to deal with things if I pretend it happened to someone else. So sometimes before I go to bed, before the bullets, I think about that girl that I used to see at Big Panty concerts, and I pretend she is the one who picked up the lighter. I picture her putting the cigarette between her lips and raising the lighter just under her nose. She's doing it the exact same way I did. She closes her eyes and brings her thumb down. She bends her neck to get even closer, the exact same way. And then it's her hand that erupts and her face that gets sprayed and her world that darkens. But soon the bullets are fired to put me out of my misery. And another day is upon me.

DON'T LOOK AT ME! I am the burning bush. I am the vision. I am the walrus, goo goo goo joob!

Ten Things I Didn't Bother to Put in my Diary

1. THURSDAY: I bought two Paydays at Casey's. It was a dollar eighty-nine. I thought that was a lot for two candy bars, they weren't king-sized or anything, but that was actually the price of just one. With tax the two candy bars cost four dollars and six cents. I paid with a five dollar bill and said, Can I take the pennies out of the pennies cup? Every Casey's has a penny cup. You could tell the woman thought taking six was an abuse of the system, but the cup was filled with pennies and I've left plenty of pennies in the cups over the years, although not at this particular Casey's. I considered telling her I was on a bicycle and didn't want the coins jingling in my pocket. There were several nickels in the change cup and even one dime just to give you an idea of how much change there was, but I only took pennies; counting out to six one by one. If I added spaces and signed this Billy Collins, you would say this is the best poem Billy Collins ever wrote, the old man is back in form!, and you would give me a million dollars for the poem, which I would exchange for pennies and spread them around to all the Casey's I bike to.

2. MONDAY: Watch one of the Criterion movies I've been waiting to see, Niagara. Marilyn Monroe in one of those, oh-I-kind-of-get-it-now performances and some other actor, Jean Peters, who is compelling and pretty and looks amazing in wet shorts climbing out of the Niagara River, so much so I googled her and saw that she had been married to Howard Hughes, which felt about right. It's 9pm and I bring Sophie out for a-pissin' and then go to bed on the early side.

3. MONDAY: Went down to meet Jakob to split wood. Took Jeep because I was concerned about getting back to meet the chimney sweep. When the sweep texted he had arrived, I drove up from the creek and I have to say I liked my entrance: red checked mackinaw, Carhartt hat with the label askew, overalls, high Muck boots, and a Gator bed full of split wood. The chimney sweep was unpacking his brushes and tools and I asked where he keeps the small children, but he didn't answer. Despite that, he was very chatty and asked a lot of questions. He asked about the amount of acreage on the farm which most local people know not to do because it's offensive, like asking a city person how much money they have. The chimney sweep asked what year our house was built, how I mow the lawn, how we finish the cattle, how old Abe was when he died, how old Natty is now, if and how well she gets around, did we get our insert stove from Benson Stone, do I remember who from Benson Stone installed the insert stove, did Natty also get her insert stove from Benson Stone, where do we process our cattle, do I think the processer might take some of the meat without telling me, have I noticed how all these dialysis places started springing up just at the same time doctors started prescribing a lot of medication for high blood pressure, do I hunt, had Abe been a hunter, and when did I think I would know if we would have extra beef to sell him. He did our chimney pretty quickly and said it had been a relatively easy job because I did a good job rotating the wood. I do spend some time every fall rotating the wood pile, and I nearly blushed when he made that observation. I probably thought about this compliment a dozen times throughout the rest of the day, like when a college professor tells you you've made a good point in a class discussion.

4. SUNDAY: I cry during the karaoke scene in Lost in Translation. I also cry at the end of Bicycle Thieves and at some point in every episode of Derry Girls (first two seasons only) which is embarrassing because I am usually sitting with wife and slash or daughter, neither of whom are crying. I cry while watching that YouTube video made by a town in Italy, which gathered one thousand musicians to play Learning to Fly in an effort to get the Foo Fighters to notice them. I cry when I listen to the Talking Heads song, "This Must be the Place" because of the line, "Did I find you or you find me," and I cry at the Guided by Voices song, "Don't Stop Now," but not the album version; the demo version on "King Shit and the Golden Boys" which is just a guitar being strummed and Robert Pollard's voice at its most clangingly lonely. He sounds depleted and ready for bed. I get choked up at the sentiment "Surrender, surrender, but don't give yourself away," in the Cheap Trick song, just as I was moved as an adolescent by 38 Special's notion that one should, "Hold on loosely, but [not] let go." I never cried at that per se, but apparently the strategy of backing off while still hanging in there resonates powerfully to me, and has so all my life. I cry during the Dumb Starbucks episode of Nathan For You because I am touched by how popular the shop becomes and how excited everyone is about it. It's the montage of the broadcast news reports that gets me sobbing. It also happens during the montage of news broadcasts during the episode where Nathan fakes a viral video of a pig rescuing a goat from drowning. Apparently I am also an emotional sucker for a good montage.

5. TUESDAY: Dreamt the small apartment Molly and I lived in was filled with workmen and animals and family and I was complaining to one of the workmen about the amount of commotion, but in a light hearted, whaddya-gonna-do kind of way. While making coffee at 6:20am I changed the kitchen garbage bag, emptied the dishwasher, and put the sink dishes into the now empty dishwasher. I also cleaned the cat box where I accidentally, he first time I believe, due to an error in judgment regarding how I was holding the plastic grocery sack, touched a cat turd and got some on my finger. Then, in an attempt to assess the damage, I thought to sniff the be-turded finger and made two more errors: the second and more damaging error was to misjudge the distance between my finger and nose and making contact, the first error was deciding to sniff my finger in the first place. All in all, by the time I was scrubbing my hands and face at the kitchen sink, I felt pretty discouraged bout the morning slash my whole life.

6. WEDNESDAY: Drive to Byron and sit in the Quick Lube waiting room where they had "NBC's Morning Shit" on the teevee loudly. It is beyond my comprehension that anyone would slash CAN willingly subject themselves to this. Go to Rockford for last minute slash all of my Christmas presents. Start at Kohl's. Why? I hate that place and there is literally nothing on the shelves that anyone would want. Go to Bed Bath and Beyond. Strike two. Go to Binny's Liquors. There I spend close to 200 dollars but not on any gifts, just on a bunch of booze so I can make fun drinks for my kids and nieces and nephews. Later, after dinner, I try to read but hear a flapping against the window. I saw it was a robin. It was pressed up against the glass so that I could see its color. Never saw a bird this late in the day before and it was really flapping around, and then I realized the cat had him in his jaws. I tried to open the window and attempt some sort of rescue but the bird started squeaking and then the cat ran off with him. It was actually pretty disturbing.

7. SATURDAY: My ten favorite chapters in "Moby-Dick" in order.
1. Chapter 94: A Squeeze of the Hand.
2. Chapter 35: The Mast-Head.
3. Chapter 89: Fast-Fish and Loose-Fish.
4. Chapter 54 The Town-Ho's Story.
5. Chapter 96 The Try-Works.
6. Tie between Chapter 64: Stubb's Supper. & Chapter 65: The Whale as a Dish.
7. Chapter 13: Wheelbarrow.
8. Chapter 112: The Blacksmith.
9. Chapter 32: Cetology.
10. Chapter 93: The Castaway.

8. TUESDAY: Drove to Rockford and got a gyro at Nick's which I've been thinking about since Saturday when we went to Oasis with Julia and Fin Lee and I didn't get one. Sat in the car and woofed it down. No fork so had to use hand to catch the eloping onions when I bit into the pita. Was given six napkins which seemed excessive, almost insulting, but turned out to be just enough to cover me. Made me feel seen by the people at Nick's. Drove to Pinnon's IGA and was already happy somehow just being in that place, unchanged for decades, and seeing it so lively. I said, Libman, 25 pounds, and the butcher said, "That's the one we ate." And the other butcher said, "Libman, yeah, we cooked it and ate it. You prepaid, right?" All I could come up with was, "You would have done a better job than I'm going to do," which ended things. I appreciate good banter and they were prepared and had home field advantage, but still I could have done better. I started looking at the hot sauces and then the guy brought out the bird, which was actually 26.5 pounds. I headed over to the checkout counter and they have two registers and the crowd was sort of all over the place, and one of the women waved me over. I said, "I don't want to cut," and she said, "They should be paying attention." I said, "I really love this place." And she gave me a funny look, and I said, "It really makes me happy you're still around, just being here. I bet since you work here it doesn't make you happy." And she said, "Not today." Considered going to Nicholson Hardware just to have hit all my favorite Rockford places, but had the turkey warming in the back seat so drove home.

9. SUNDAY: Beau Wilder shows up, then Sue and Spencer. It's drizzling, "chippy-chippy" like they said in Guatemala: steady but light and not too bad if you have a raincoat, which we all did. Head out into the woods and end up walking the mud and undergrowth for almost three hours. We find no morels. It's not a terrible time, but kind of disappointing. Beau and Sue can talk about trees by name. Where I say, "Let's look by that big one over there," they say, "Let's check that ash next to the maple." Beau can also recognize birds by their songs. He will suddenly say, "Shhh…. It's a scarlet tanager! Hear it? A scarlet tanager!" Then he takes out his phone and plays a scarlet tanager song back to the real scarlet tanager, who starts singing louder at the phone, and even begins to buzz-bomb us looking for the other scarlet tanager. To me it seems mean, plus half the time I thought he was saying "Scarlet Johansson" so I was doubly confused.

10. FRIDAY: Dreamt that I was on a big, weeklong bike ride that I had done many times, but somehow every night we stayed in the same college dorm. I had gotten back from one ride and all my stuff had been moved from one dorm room to another. When I got up, Molly told me I would have to do all the morning chores because she had to teach yoga and hadn't even, "written a see-quinz." I said, that's every Friday. I walked the dog. I was irritated but it was quite lovely out. Bitter cold but pretty: frost covering everything, shimmery white on the ground and treetops, hazy sun punching the mist coming off the creek. Sophie's shit met the esthetic challenge and was magnificent in girth and hue. Opened the chickens and gave them water. Drove to the university. One portfolio in mailbox in Beeswing Hall. Box of cookies on the beggar table by the secretary, which I gave the once over but then ate none of. A win! Fingers feel weird—pinky keeps going numb on right hand. Went to Potbelly. Guy passed me near chain link fence and said, Isn't this a perfect day? I said, Great! Dumb answer but he caught me off guard. I wish I had said, The sun is very pleasant but it's a tad cold for me. Got in line at Potbelly which was short. A guy very stoked to see me was in front of me in line. "Mr. Libman!" I did the, Wow it's been awhile, now tell me your name again? Carson. We caught up and then said goodbye. Because Carson's order was slightly complicated (two sandwiches, and when he told the sandwich maker to put the peppers "on the side" for the second sandwich, I figured it was for a girlfriend,) this meant he had to stay in the "directions bay" for a bit, so we were compelled to do more "catching up." He asked about what I've been up to (still teaching) and he corrected me on something I misheard (graduating this May, not last May). Then we again said how nice it had been to see each other and he moved on to the register. My sandwich directions are easy (everything, please) so when I was done and Carson was still at the register, (on-the-side-peppers slows everyone down because they have to be procured and packaged by the cashier ladies,) we were compelled to again reiterate how nice this visit had been, and—I suppose to differentiate this farewell from the previous two—we shook hands. At no point did

Carson ever seem even remotely familiar to me, and after shaking his hand, I realized it wasn't just my pinky that was numb, but my whole right hand. My shoulder was starting to feel funny too.

The Shapes of Places

Her teacher must have been unhappy on that day–he was always unhappy. He had been about 200 years old, never smiled, and when he read out loud to the class you could smell his coffee and cigarette breath no matter where you sat. But Alice had decided she might cheer him up with a recent discovery, one that had made her happy. So she walked up to his desk and told him, "America is like a chicken."

He looked up from his grading—he had spit balls in the corners of his mouth which made Alice lick her own lips. He said, "If you mean a country that isn't afraid to defend its way of life even overseas; a country that puts the needs of its common citizens ahead of the rich, feeds its poor, shelters its indigent. If you think those are the ideals of chickens, then yes, I suppose we are chickens!"

She hadn't meant the country was a chicken, just that it looked like a chicken; with Maine being its head, Florida and Texas the feet, and all the western states puffing up and out like the body. Washington state even had a little tail that might look like feathers if you used imagination. She could have explained that to her teacher, but something about the deliberate way his head turned back made her decide not to pursue it.

The experience didn't dampen her enthusiasm for looking at maps. The first gift she ever gave her husband was a corkboard map of the world. Marcel had just been promoted from the PR department to a Coordinatorship and would be traveling all over the globe. It was Alice's idea that he should stick a plastic pin in every place he visited so that he could show people the map and say, "This is where I've been."

He was gracious about the map and hung it on the wall of their house, though he never did use any of the plastic pushpins that she had bought for him. Now she realized that to a man like Marcel—a man who had moved with his military family as a kid, a man who had traveled all over the globe and had visited nearly everywhere—to a man like that, sticking pins into a corkboard wasn't too amusing. But he had hung the map as a courtesy to her. Whenever Alice went into his den to get a new typewriter ribbon or more paper she would pause at the map and it reminded her that even though Marcel was somewhere out in the world, there was something to be said about being where she was, in Denver, which on this map was pretty much smack dab in the center of the whole world. She let her eyes wander over the familiar shapes, the deep blues and light oranges and yellows, until it all blurred into an alluring panoply that spun like a pinwheel.

Marcel had offered to give her the big office after they were married since she was still freelancing for the Denver Post Sunday Supplement. But she had a different idea and set up her office in the back half of the narrow attic. She told him it was because of the window, that she needed a view to spark her imagination, that even a tiny view of another house was better than nothing. Actually, Alice had plans for the whole of the attic, and when the time was right, she would use that front space as the children's nursery. She would work on her articles while the children napped, and their gurgling and gentle snoring would be her inspiration.

She got two cribs from her sister who had four children and recently declared herself, "out of the baby business." Each crib went under an opposing slope of the roof so that the dormer was between them. For good luck, Alice scattered toys and stuffed animals around the floor like seeds. She hung maps on the walls, too: maps of the states and maps of national parks and maps of foreign countries. There was even a map of the solar system with the orbits of the planets around the sun represented by dotted lines so that the universe looked like a pile of fried eggs.

And she waited. She drove Marcel to the airport, ticked off the days, wrote her stories for the Sunday Supplement, shoveled the walks and cleaned the house, and weeks later picked him up from the airport. When she got stuck on a story or needed a boost of confidence she went into the nursery and read her articles out loud and imagined the faces of her children listening in rapt attention. But the cribs stayed empty. Alice looked at the maps while she waited, letting her eyes rise and fall along the jagged borders and fluttering rivers.

This continent looks like an ice cream cone, she would say pointing to Africa. She stood in front of the window so that she could be between the cribs. *And these islands, the Philippines, they look like a dog that's been told to heel. And see this, the way Norway and Sweden touch? It looks like a man diving head first off a diving board. See his head, and the way his hands stretch out in front of him? Now children, look carefully. Which country is shaped like a chicken?*

MARCEL ONLY LIKED TOAST and butter in the mornings, so when he was home, Alice got up with him to make it while he showered. It was the sort of life she wished she could be sick of.

"Hey, party rye," he said, settling into his chair and eyeing his plate. "Not bad. So what are you working on now?" He took his first bite of toast.

"I got a hot one," Alice said, settling in across the table. "A feature on this woman who works at a drive-through window at a Hanger Burger. The woman signs. You know: sign language?"

He nodded, chewing. "I heard about it, once or twice," he said, smiling.

"Well, anyway, apparently she signs for deaf customers and now deaf people go out of their way to use this Hanger Burger's drive-through."

Marcel had a bulky body of odd proportions, small bird-like legs and arms, but a big barrel chest and a large head which he kept unfashionably mustached. "She speaks English too, right?" he asked brushing crumbs from the corners of his lips. "Or do you need a translator for the interview?"

"She can hear, Marcel. She works in a drive-through window She probably has a deaf relative or something. You can read all about it in next Sun-dee Denver Post Bullshit Supplee-ment."

"Well, unfortunately I'll be in Egypt already with a new group. But by all means, save the article for me." He grinned at her and Alice made a face.

Alice had been writing a story on The Foundation when she first met Marcel. It was summer and she had been dressed professionally for the interview, a sleeveless but tasteful outfit, her feet in trendy flats and hair cut short. She had just lost six pounds to a flu virus a month before and so was feeling unusually confident. Marcel *was* the PR department then, and when he met her at the door and shook her hand, she made sure to grip firmly and maintain eye contact. He walked her through the lobby and Alice felt light and regal, like a gazelle. He had a slight southern accent and was handsome and Alice knew she was already in love, but felt oddly relaxed and confident. She felt an unusual kind of pressure pushing her along the corridor, a press of the inevitable just at her back.

They sat across from each other in his cubicle and Alice asked questions and Marcel answered them, needlessly projecting his voice towards her microcassette recorder as though she were taping an interview to be broadcast. "We take young, gifted students," he said. "And give them an opportunity to travel and see parts of the world...." And as the interview progressed the office chairs rolled closer until Marcel and Alice's knees actually touched. They didn't bother to slide back, as if it had been inevitable that they would get married and sit at breakfast and eat toast together.

Marcel dipped his crust into the jar of orange marmalade. "Do you think the Hanger Burger has its own set of signs, you know, that might be different from Taco Glutton or Chicken Anonymous? Like a special sign for Jumbo Jet with cheese?" He held his hands in front of him as if he were gripping an enormous burger.

"Maybe like..." Alice bared her teeth and took huge bites in the air.

Marcel mimed dropping his burger and wiping at the table with a napkin. Alice pretended to vomit, silently heaving onto the table.

"I'll let you know when you get back," she told him.

"Well," Marcel said. "After the Egypt trip, I'm going to be meeting a group in Chile, so I won't be around for a while."

Here is where your father is, she would say to the babies, pointing to the maps. *Chile is this long red country. What does it look like to you?*

"I wouldn't go to Chile if you paid me," She said abruptly. "Take a cold, hard look at that country," she said. "It's stupid looking. Like one strong wave from the Pacific could wash it away."

"What?" He leaned back and looked at her with an exaggerated squint.

"It's a dumb looking country," she said. "Long and narrow, like a bean stalk. I say give the land to Argentina, except the top which should go to Peru. And then get rid of Bolivia and make that part of Peru, so that Peru and Argentina would look like two hair ribbons, tied in the middle."

"What do you have against Bolivia?" he asked.

"Terrible human rights abuses," she said matter of factly.

"Right. Well, maybe the Sunday Supplement could assign you to do a big exposé. You know, where does the Generalissimo go to unwind after a long day of," he made quote signs in the air, "abusing human rights."

She sneered. It surprised her to feel stung by the remark since it was the type of joke she made all the time about her articles. Today though it felt like he was being ungrateful. She felt for a second like reminding him that it was her article, which had been picked up by two news wires and run internationally, which had made him look so good in the first place and gotten him out of the PR department and into the traveling Coordinatorship.

He reached across the table and put his hand on her arm. "You're mad, aren't you?"

"You're just so smug," she told him, though she didn't feel half as indignant as a second earlier. "You're so sure that I don't have any good ideas."

"I thought you were kidding about Chili. Okay, let's give it to Peru."

"I *was* kidding. Forget about it." She slid her arm out from his and took the plate and brushed the crumbs into the sink.

DESPITE HERSELF, ALICE WAS very impressed with the Hanger Burger drive-through woman. Her name was Clare, and she was articulate and good humored. She was many years older than Alice, and had a bright face and the top of her head was covered in tight grey curly hair like a Q-tip. They sat in a booth together, under a model airplane suspended from the ceiling on fishing wire, both sipping free milkshakes—the gift of an assistant manager who understood the benefits of free publicity.

"At first it seemed crazy that people would. . . . But I guess it's a novelty, ordering from a window, and everyone likes to do it . . ." Clare trailed off into laughter, something she did regularly. Alice liked her right away because she had a nice sense of herself as being somewhat ridiculous, but also able to make people happy. She let Clare talk and demonstrate the signs, but Alice had no idea how she would remember them or describe them to her readers.

"This is for pie and this is ice cream cone," Clare said into Alice's recorder. "And this is what they use for milkshake . . . chocolate . . . vanilla . . . and this," she made a whirling gesture with her finger, "means both flavors, mixed." Clare burst out laughing so joyfully that Alice laughed too.

The story took almost no time to write, and Alice found herself smiling as she transcribed the tape. Sometimes she would repeat the sign, swirling her finger in front of her face. She liked watching the rapid movements of her hand through the haze of light from the window.

"Clare Rangell provides a unique service to the deaf community of Denver," she read to the cribs. She imagined the big eyes of her children listening to her, hanging on to her every word.

What does deaf mean? one of them might ask. *What's a community? What's a language?*

She looked at Chile on the map. As soon as her own children were born she would start to school them. She would surround them with books and educational toys, and never let them watch television. If she hadn't had so much television as a kid she might have gone on one of those trips with Marcel's Foundation.

Show me the two states that are dancing with each other. That's right, Wisconsin and Michigan. See how Michigan is reaching over to give Wisconsin a twirl?

Who can tell me the name of the little island that looks like a boomerang? Cuba! That's right! Aren't you smart! So much smarter than mama. Now look carefully, which country looks like a boot kicking a soccer ball?

"THIS IS GOOD BREAD," Marcel said, chewing a piece of raisin toast.

"I always say," Alice told him. "If you want good bread, you have to take the time to buy the prepackaged mix and turn on the machine."

"Really? I thought you found the machine absurd."

"I did. I do. But what the hell? The bread's good. I'm flexible that way, don't you think? Besides, I've made bread by hand before, practically sprained my wrist kneading it, and you didn't say a word about that bread."

He once told her she had a rare gift for wounding herself on the ugly unintended edge of any compliment paid to her. "So how did your interview go with the deaf woman?"

"I told you she's not deaf. And actually it went really well. A nice change of pace. Did you know sign language has different gestures in other parts of the world?"

Marcel considered this. "That makes sense," he said. "Since it just abstracts whatever grammar is being spoken."

"I had never thought about that before. This Clare's really smart. She just learned sign language because she was interested in it. Isn't that odd? It's like a hobby."

Marcel snorted. "So what is she doing at Hanger Burger if she's so smart?"

"I don't know. No breaks. Not rich. Not gifted. You know, I've been thinking about filling out one of them there applications myself."

"For Hanger Burger?"

"For Hanger Burger," she repeated. "No. For one of your Foundation travel grant dealy-bobbers. I've got an idea for something I could examine. I'm going to fill out an application and insist you evaluate me. It's not fair that the program wasn't around when I was young."

"Sure it was."

"You're poo-pooing even before you've heard my proposal. Listen, I think it's very new, very original. Part of this whole," she clasped her hands together, "coming together of all the disciplines that's very hot these days. I want to look at borders." She was making it up as she spoke but the more she said, the more excited she got. "I want to look at the way lines, the lines on maps, you know, randomly drawn by fallible humans and all that, how these lines have a serious concrete effect on the nature—the whole psyche—of the inhabitants."

He shook his head slightly. "Don't get you."

She leaned in and spoke rapidly. "Like I live in a box-shaped state. Colorado is just a big box with no doors. Mixed metaphor. A box with no lid, or rather, let's say a room with no door, because I like the missing door as an image. I feel closed in by these random lines around me. Now if I had lived in Nevada, see, can you picture Nevada? It's like a box too, only with a trap door on the bottom. So if I had been in Nevada I might have gotten out. Slid out through the bottom."

"You'd have slid out of the bottom of Nevada?"

"I'm not saying this is true for everyone, just those of us who are particularly suggestible." She felt a little tugging, a slight little tremor of the inevitable; she had started out joking but she had gotten on the right track.

"I saw that box labeled Colorado and I thought, 'I'm in that box.' I know, I'm back to the box imagery again; I'll choose door or box and get it all cleaned up by the time I'm ready to submit my application." She winked at him. "Didn't know I could think so deeply, did you?"

"Alice, why are you so insecure? You're romanticizing these trips and what....what I do. Come along on one if you really want. It's a lot of trying to get drunken teenagers back to the hotel and finding restaurants and phones, but by all means, come along—"

"I'm not going to *come along*. I'm going to study the effects of geography on a population."

"Okay." He chuckled. "You need a vacation anyway, I guess."

"I'll start working on the application—"

"You don't need to fill out—"

"I'll start working on the application and then we'll find the appropriate country from your immediate itinerary . . ." Her voice trailed off and she smiled. "I'll check out a guidebook from the library. This is going to end up being fun!"

THEY WERE WALKING ON a narrow cobblestone road in the middle of the afternoon and although the sky was blue and the sun bright, the passage between two walled courtyards was narrow and deeply shadowed. Alice had picked a restaurant from the guidebook, and Marcel was enthusiastic about a quiet, late lunch. It was their first meal together since arriving the day before. They turned a corner on to a much wider street, which was also empty.

"Here." Marcel pointed to a small building covered in vines. An open door led to a narrow room of tables. All the chairs were empty, and Marcel chose a table close to the street.

"This is pretty much what the guidebook said," Alice declared with great satisfaction. "Right on the money again."

Once they were sitting, a man in a bright orange pill-box hat and overalls appeared from behind a curtain. He carried a hunk of bread, torn at both ends, and wordlessly put it between them on the table. Alice smiled at the man, but he was already retreating through the curtain.

"That's the taciturn efficiency this little bistro is known for," she said with mock seriousness. Then, brightening, "The book said to be sure and come early. The guys who wrote it are so smart."

"That's why they're at Harvard," Marcel murmured.

"They say to stay away from the lamb dishes," she continued. "People around here often try to pass off goat as lamb."

"What have you seen so far?" Marcel leaned back in his chair and folded his arms.

"It's been just perfect! The people are gregarious and I adore the lovely lilting quality of the language. The 'ahs' and the 'ehs.' It's like . . ." She opened her mouth as if someone was taking a throat culture.

Marcel looked away. "Alice, not to criticize, but don't you find that all a little cliched—the friendly locals and the mellifluous language? It's a peeve of mine that some travelers seem to only find exactly what the guidebooks tell them they're going to find. I mean, you're treating this like an auditor going through someone's tax return. Where's the satisfaction in that?"

"What . . ." Alice paused for no particular reason and then began again. "What exactly are you criticizing? My guidebook?"

"No no . . ."

Alice held up a hand as the waiter returned with two bowls of a murky yellow soup and spoons wrapped in paper towels. Alice spoke the sounds recommended in the guidebook for expressing gratitude. The man nodded curtly before leaving.

"I need to apologize," Marcel unwrapped his spoon and began polishing the bowl-end with the paper towel. "It's not you. It's the students. I'm noticing a tendency . . . every trip it's a little worse. Maybe it's because of cable or the Internet. . . . They find the Israelis brusque but spirited and the Japanese distant but exotic." He stirred and blew once across his soup. "There's a descriptive word for you: Exotic. You're a writer. Tell me what exotic is supposed to mean."

"Oh, well. We don't got none of them On Language columns in the Sun-dee Supplement."

Marcel looked up. Alice had a pinched look on her face like an old dowager. She had her lips pompously pushed out and was vigorously wiping her spoon, in a broad imitation of what he had just done. Marcel chuckled.

"These trips are stressful, sweetie. I'm sorry," he said quickly. "You know I think you're a great writer. It doesn't matter that you only write for that paper. I was just saying you could come up with some different reactions to the place. But you've only been here a day or so and I don't know what I was expecting. But you shouldn't be so insecure, you know? One snippy remark from me shouldn't set you off. We all know you're as smart as any of these kids."

"Really? Smart as the kids?"

"Don't do that," Marcel put his spoon down. "Don't go out of your way to be offended."

Alice took a mouthful of the soup. It was unlike any soup she had tasted before, though it had a vague familiar flavor she couldn't place. But it was good. She wiped her lips with the paper towel. "Listen Marcel, this ain't exactly untrod ground we're standing on. It's not my fault I've arrived here after thousands of years of tourism."

"I'll tell you what you should be examining," he said. "And it isn't the way shapes of places alter the inhabitants. It's the how language dictates the way travelers *see* a place. A reaction formation . . . you know it? Every country on the planet has all these associations from the movies and television. No one can see anything fresh anymore. A scene cuts to a Japanese street and then you hear a gong. A gong strike with lots of sustain that fades out. Now it's in our head, and we go to Japan, and it's. . . Gonnnnggg. . . ." He made a quick raspberry. Then he picked up his spoon and pointed to her. "I've an idea: You come with me on the next trip, only I don't tell you where we're going, blindfold you on the plane and make you wear headphones with music until we leave the hotel, and then let's see what you find. Let's see how you describe it."

She slammed her spoon on to the table, which made a very disappointing little thud on the soft wood. "You want me to get it wrong."

"There's nothing to get wrong. You just react. And we see what happens without pre-associations. I'm just riffing with you here, brainstorming."

"Aha!" Alice shouted. She recognized those phrases from the Foundation's literature she had read years ago. "You can't think for yourself either. You just want me to go out and try to guess where I am so that when I get it wrong you can feel better about yourself."

"I don't want you to guess where you are. I thought it would be interesting to come up with new descriptions without preconception. I'll give you an example. I was eating here with some of the students yesterday and we were eating this soup," he tapped the lip of the bowl with the spoon. "And one of them said it tasted like a sweet potato if you liquified it. And of course this soup is made from squash and chick peas, but he had come up with this fresh description that, while not accurate, was still useful. I mean, it does have a sweet-potatoey quality. . . ."

He's been here before. She pushed her soup away. It did taste like whipped sweet potatoes; it wasn't exotic at all.

"Okay," he said looking at her bowl. "I didn't mean to upset you. I'll pay for the soups and we can go back to the hotel."

Alice pushed her chair back, grabbed the guidebook off the table and walked toward the door. Marcel was calling either to her or the waiter, she couldn't tell, and she lost the sound after a few steps down the shadowy street. She took a turn and then the next turn, landing her feet as gingerly as possible on the uneven cobblestones, until the street opened up onto a bright and open square. She didn't know where she was now, didn't recognize this square even though she had seen many like it, either here or on TV, she wasn't sure. A large group of men and women walked into a darkened café with an open entrance. Even from across the square Alice could hear raucous talking and laughing.

The café was smokey, packed with tables from wall to wall. Alice walked around looking for an empty seat, and she noticed that everyone was dressed in strange costumes, made from a senseless mix of burlap and silk. The faces of the patrons were hidden by elaborate head-gear; hats topped with hideous, rabid looking creatures; papier-mâché wolves with bloodied chickens hanging from their mouths, foam vultures screeching into the air.

Since there were no available tables, Alice chose a lone chair against a wall and sat down. She opened her guide-book on her lap, even though it was much too dark to read. She didn't want to gawk at the costumes too much, but she let herself listen to the cacophony of the room. A waitress handed her a coffee in a tall clear glass. The glass had no handle, and because Alice didn't have a table, she was forced to hold it in her hands. It was very hot, and she found that all she could do was grip it across the top where there was no liquid. The language around her didn't seem at all like the one she had been listening to earlier on the trip. This language had strange clicking and coughing sounds in it; it was completely unfamiliar, but the more she listened the more she could sense familiar rising and falling patterns that gave way to meaning.

"You're pretentious," one of the voices said.

"No, you're pretentious," said another. Several people laughed.

Alice listened earnestly but kept her eyes on the glass as if it were a complicated puzzle she was trying to solve. Although she was not able to break the babble into dis-cernible chunks, she seemed to be catching everything that was said.

"This brand of cigarette is not my favorite, but for now, it'll do." Was that right? She'd read that it took months of immersion just to pick up even the basics of a language. Certainly she didn't have the innate ability to learn this quickly.

She was vaguely aware of being watched by faces under animal masks. The conversation in the café was getting louder, and more animated.

"You are henpecking me!" said a man gaily. And yet the man did not say "hen pecking," but a clucking phrase that could not be translated directly; bird-bothering, or something similar.

"I would I were thy bird," said a voice, using the same word for "bird" included in the "henpecking" phrase. More laughter.

"Tweet tweet! Sweets for the sweet!" There was howling and the man pounded the table gleefully.

"No, no, no," came a different voice, much closer to her. "I mean that woman and her coffee."

Alice looked up. She felt trapped. All the faces were pointed at her, rows and rows of floating eyes and fangs and whiskers. She put both hands tightly around the glass and felt the heat in her palms.

"Tell us please," a booming male voice shouted. "Does she drink coffee, or does she represent a woman drinking coffee?" Howling laughter soared throughout the café and Alice lowered her eyes and attempted to sip at the scalding hot liquid.

"I recognize that gesture," said a timid voice, "as that of a woman drinking coffee."

"Is the cup half empty or half full?" asked another.

"No, no wait," said the booming voice. "The cup is the apple, and she is Eve; look how she struggles. Don't do it! Resist!"

Alice tipped the glass against her lips and a burning spilled across her mouth. She locked her lips closed and forced herself to swallow.

"She is not a pipe," one voice declared, to actual applause and cheers from the others.

She went back for another sip, which was no easier but she was at least more prepared for the searing on her tongue. Eyes focused on the glass, thinking only of drinking, the voices fell back into the foreign tongue that was incomprehensible to her. She tried concentrating, but all she could hear was a sea of strange sounds and words that didn't seem connected to the sounds she'd understood so recently; now there was something guttural, hissing about the language. The abrupt change disquieted her and she got up to find the waitress so she could pay for her drink and leave. The animal-hatted people, as though on cue from Alice, all began rising from their chairs and moving in groups of two or three towards the door. They were leaving half-finished drinks and plates with green leafy vegetables still steaming. Since no one seemed to be paying for anything, Alice put her glass on the ground and followed out the door.

The crowd was moving quickly across the square toward the sound of a train whistle. They rounded a corner to an old antique-looking locomotive that was motionless although there didn't seem to be a station. The townspeople were climbing makeshift wooden steps to board the passenger cars. Alice had no idea if this was standard activity in this town, some sort of custom, or maybe it was a rare celebration of some kind. She had not read about this in the guidebook but she followed the crowd into the train.

People were scrambling for seats, which were quickly becoming scarce. Alice saw a bench with only two old women on it. They weren't wearing any masks but were both wrapped in red and yellow shawls and seemed to be having an animated conversation with each other. As soon as they saw Alice approach, one shifted to the aisle, so that the empty seat was now in the middle. When Alice paused, confused, they both began to pat the space between and nod at her.

As soon as she sat, the one on her left patted her arm and made a cooing noise. Her hand felt soft, almost powdery. Alice looked over the head of other woman to the window and was surprised to see that the train had already begun moving. Low rock walls were going by quickly, and she was overcome with a fluttering in her stomach. She was afraid for a second that she might leap into the air with joy. The old women, as if sensing her concern, took hold of her elbows and gripped tightly. Alice was grateful for the contact, for the feel of their hands on her arms, and she flipped her guidebook open to the front page that had a map of the world.

"Look," she said pointing. "This is us. See?" The women looked together but did not react. Alice looked from one to the other and their faces were reflections of the same indifference. "The three of us," Alice made the whirling Hanger Burger gesture with her finger. "Here," she pointed to the appropriate shape on the map.

The two women began to laugh quietly and shake their heads no. The one on her left imitated the swirling gesture. The one on her right brought her arms together like wings and flapped them a few times. "Cluck cluck," she said. She pointed to the United States.

"Yes yes," Alice said excitedly. "It does look like a chicken, doesn't it?" The other woman now was flapping her arms like wings and clucked a few times and they both laughed and nodded.

Alice could barely contain herself. "Now...which one...which continent looks like an ice cream cone?" Alice held her fist to her mouth as though holding a cone and stuck her tongue out to lick the invisible ice cream. The woman on her left pointed to Africa and Alice nodded and smiled.

Before she could ask another question, the woman on her right pressed her finger into the guidebook, pointing to a drawing of railroad tracks that ran across some of the shapes, over a number of borders. Alice didn't know the names of the countries that the tracks ran over, but it ran like a zipper across much of the page, and she watched the old woman's finger as it slowly traced the route, rising and falling with the unexpected humps of geography, through one country, and then the next, and the next, and the next.

Shocker in Gloomtown

S tan had only come to the cookout to make an "effort," which is what his wife said he needed to do more of if he had any chance of getting back with her. Socializing was an obligation since the divorce, made him feel like a child being forced to smile pleasantly with spinster aunties or distant cousins. He picked at the food on his plate—carrots and a mound of ranch dip—gamely chatting with his host.

"I'm not just saying 'I've given up on getting grandchildren' just to trick the gods into giving me some," Beatrice said to him. "I've really *given up*."

"Yep," he answered. It wasn't just that Beatrice's daughter Sofia was sitting at the same picnic table and in earshot making Stan uncomfortable, it was also the unfairness of it all: if Ferrol hadn't left him, she would be the one talking to Beatrice and Stan could just be eating.

"You don't know what it's like, you and Ferrol with your dozen grandkids," Beatrice continued. "What's the actual number?"

"Eh," Stan paused to wipe his brow with his napkin. "Chuck is twelve now, so. . . ."

"You do know how many grandkids you have, don't you Stan? You're not that blasé about it, are you?"

He knew, he just had to think a second. There was Chuck of course, and then the two boys born after that, then a

91

girl, then the foster girl from Russia who was adopted, and then there was another boy and a baby girl with a birthday coming up.

"Seven," he told her, holding up the fingers on which he had just done the counting.

"Leave Mr. Overly alone, mom," Sofia said, giving him a jokey clap on the shoulder. Sofia had been engaged to Stan's son many years back, and he had always liked her.

"How long are you visiting?" he asked her.

"I've returned home. Didn't Mrs. Overly tell you?"

"We're not in close communication, lately," he mumbled as Beatrice left for other guests. Stan felt for Sofia an intense gratitude, bordering on fealty.

Sofia said, "I've been back in Red Chief for almost a year now." She made a face. "Gloomtown. I'm sober and working at the nursing home. I'm living with my parents until I get some money saved. It's actually not so bad."

Sofia had an inviting way about her. Something about her expressive lips and eyes always reminded Stan of the way friendly, talking animals were depicted in children's books, like the plucky, heroic pony who perseveres against the bigger horses and wins the day. "In fact," she said putting her hand on his shoulder again, "I'd like to show you something if you've got a second. In the basement."

The Conovers had an endless supply of basement furniture, often given away when the church put out an "Action Item of Mercy" in the bulletin. If one of the migrants from Mexico had a baby, Beatrice and Rupert could be counted on for a crib or bassinette, and when three refugees from Sudan came to Red Chief, the Conovers provided a kitchen table and a sectional couch.

"Watch out for all the clutter," Sofia told Stan, guiding him between an upturned coffee table and a tall wardrobe.

Sofia's shirt was backless and Stan could just make out in the dim light a tattoo on her lower back: some sort of angry, screeching hawk with large talons. Stan remembered suddenly hearing his son Louis describing this tattoo to a police sergeant when filling out the order of restraint. Apparently she had broken into Louis's home but had only scrubbed the tubs and sinks, and on another occasion she had organized a closet full of suits so that his jackets hung with matching pants, over which she placed coordinating neckties that she'd purchased herself. Stan had not believed these charges, or rather he believed them in some abstract way, since the Sofia Conover he knew seemed like a reasonable person to him; a little clingy perhaps, but pleasant. He just didn't understand why his son had to call the cops in the first place—she was obviously harmless.

"Just in the corner here," she called to Stan.

Behind a roll top desk was a four-poster bed with rumpled sheets and an untucked blanket. On a bedside table was a wine bottle with a candle sticking out. Sofia struck a match and lit it before hopping on the bed.

"This frame came over from England with my mother's family," she told him. "It's generations old. A real family heirloom. The mattress is new, but isn't the wood beautiful?"

Running his hand on the nearest post, Stan nodded politely.

Sofia continued, "It's much nicer than modern, flimsy frames. It always bugged me the way mom relegates anything with character to the basement. Sit, give it a try."

"No, thank you."

"This is also the bed," she continued. "You might be interested in knowing, where your son Louis took my virginity."

"Well now, Sofia. That's not really any of my business." Stan scanned the gloom of the basement trying to find the way back to the stairs.

"It's okay, Mr. Overly. I made him do it. I took him down here because my bed upstairs made a lot of noise. We were both virgins, callow."

"I don't know anything about that," he said. Stan vaguely remembered the lawyers were very specific many years ago about not looking alarmed or making sudden movements. Or was that what you did when cornered by a bear?

"I want to preface what I'm about to propose by reminding you that I loved Louis back when we decallowed each other. I wanted to raise his children. I've accepted that it didn't happen. Someone else is raising his children, and so many of them! But when I heard about your divorce, an idea occurred to me." Sofia placed her hand on her stomach and raised her shirt slightly.

She must be mentally ill. He had to be kind now, not burst out laughing. "Sofia now, I'm flattered. Really." He tried to sound upbeat, avuncular. "It's not just the age difference either. I still love my wife and want to get back with her. Really, that's just one of about a billion reasons why we can't get married."

"I don't want to marry you Mr. Overly. I want you to get me pregnant."

Stan stopped talking. He had been looking only at her midriff since she revealed it, and now he licked his lips and spoke slowly. "I need to get back upstairs, Sofia. Right now before anyone notices we're missing."

"I'm ovulating now so this would be a good time." She raised her foot and pressed her toes into his trousers. Stan tried to back away but the boxes behind him didn't even shift.

"Optimum breeding practices dictate that you and I copulate every other day starting ten days after my last period and continue until I'm pregnant or menstruate, in which case we take a break for eight days after my cycle ends."

He gripped her ankle with his free hand, trying to nudge it, but she held firmly against him. Her toes wiggled through his pants.

"I would never take advantage—"

"I'm in my thirties, late thirties in fact, and I've thought a lot about this, Mr. Overly. I wouldn't even care if you told people providing that you don't use my name. I want to keep it a secret from my parents until you've successfully fertilized me. We should start today but I'll wait if you need to think about it."

Shoving her leg, Stan moved quickly away from the bed. "I don't need to think about it. This is . . ." He knew it was wrong to use the word crazy when talking to an actual crazy person, but he was having trouble thinking of any other word. He stubbed his ankle and hobbled back to the stairs.

Sofia called after him, "Promise me you'll think about it!"

Stan knew he would be thinking about it. That was the only thing he knew for sure.

INVITATIONS TO "THINGS" SEEMED to have multiplied since the divorce. A cookout one afternoon at the Conovers, and now this "barbecue" with his son's family the next day. He had been told to come early so as not to cross paths with Ferrol, as though he and his wife—she wasn't even officially an ex-wife yet—were two unmoored circles on a Venn diagram, destined to overlap no more. When he thought about the marriage like that, like how he might chart it on a graph at the plant: two circles, one labeled Stan and the other Ferrol, and where once they were almost on top of each other, a life filled with overlapping commonalities, now they were just floating orbs with no contact; thinking about it like that made the divorce seem real, and Stan could even feel a tightening in his throat, which, if he focused on it hard enough, he could probably turn into actual tears, though he usually didn't.

The Alluvial Estates subdivision featured streets with enormous garages, behind which squat homes cowered. Louis's walkway ran along a row of low shrubs to a single-step porch and a needlepoint cross hanging from a living room window. The screen door was unlocked and Stan could hear from the foyer his daughter in-law, Melody, and her parents whooping it up with the kids in the backyard. It took every ounce of self-control for Stan not to roll his eyes at Badge's cowboy hat hanging on the hall tree as he walked through. Melody's folks were ranchers upstate and had cattle and hogs and lots of room for children to explore. Her mother, Desirée, bought a pony just for the grandkids to ride and dug a man-made lake for them to swim in. Stan and Ferrol spent visits with their grandkids enduring stories of raft rides and owl walks and tadpole catching and bonfires with their other grandparents. If Louis had married Sofia Conover… Well, she might have been crazy but at least he and Ferrol would have just the regular amount of grandkids and in-laws with which they could reasonably compete! As it was, Ferrol refused to cede ground to Melody's parents so she sewed them clothes and made scrapbooks and cut photographs into collages as a way of remaining in their lives. For himself, Stan was just bewildered by the whole thing.

"Have you seen Chuck?" Badge asked Stan as soon as he stepped into the yard. Badge was Melody's father, the other grandpa. He was holding a basketball in the crook of his arm and had a whistle around his neck.

"Not yet," Stan told him unnecessarily as Badge brushed past him and into the house, shouting Chuck's name. Stan gave a general wave to the rest of the children. Surrounded by tall stained wood, the yard was all cement, a perfect cube sunk a foot or so into the earth, making it echoey and claustrophobic. His son Louis was piling coal into the grill near a basketball net that had been recently erected. Louis stacked coals deliberately and slowly, the way he did everything, as if one wrong move would cause the pile to collapse.

"Do kids still eat donuts? I brought a dozen from Pineway and put them on the counter inside." Stan wanted to be sure

Louis knew he hadn't come empty handed, but before he could get an answer, Badge was back in the yard, shouting.

"Won't come out until he finds some salt. It's too hot in there, Louis! Stan, tell your boy to let me pay to have a proper repairman out."

"What kind of repairman?" Stan asked.

Louis put a hand up for both of them. "Melody and I are handling it."

"Air conditioning is shot," Badge said to Stan. "Didn't you notice the heat?"

"What's wrong with it?" Stan asked. "I'll take a look."

"Bad smell and loud rumbling when they turn it on," Badge told him.

Louis grinned. "What do you know about fixing an air conditioner, dad?"

"I could look. Might be something simple and then you wouldn't have to pay—"

"Guys." When Louis put up his hand, Stan and Badge stopped talking. Settling disputes between seven children had given Louis a certain authority. "On Sunday a buddy of mine from work is coming to fix it with me. He's an electrician. So it's settled. We aren't going to be home before then anyway."

"We're taking the kids up to the ranch for the long weekend," Badge explained to Stan. "Feel free to join us. Ferrol's not coming anyway," Badge sputtered once, clearly unsure if it was okay to make the reference, before continuing. "And Louis, you wouldn't have to leave early again."

"It's all planned for Sunday, Badge."

Harboring an idea of taking a quick look at the compressor, Stan excused himself. The air conditioning unit was in the attic, just over the kid's bedrooms—a standard Alluvial Estate trick to maximize space. All the boys slept in a single room stacked in bunk beds like cordwood, and as Stan peeked in, there was Chuck on one knee, head bent. There was barely room to walk with all the clothes and junk on the floor, and not an inch of wall space not covered in basketball posters.

"Chuck? You're not. . . .praying! Are you?"

When Stan got closer he could see Chuck unlacing his shoes. He had wild curly hair and thin, tanned arms, and reeked of an innocent sort of body odor. Open in front of him was a book showing a mother pouring salt into sneakers. Chuck picked up a salt container and dumped at least half a cup into his own shoe before beginning to unlace the second.

"This is what Michael Jordan did when he was a kid," Chuck murmured.

"This is some book," Stan flipped the pages. In elaborate calligraphy was written, *To my grandson Chuck, because you love basketball and because I love you, Grandma Desirée.*

Stan felt a sudden ache in his stomach. "There are donuts downstairs. In the kitchen. I brought them. There is enough for you to have two, if you get down there fast enough."

Chuck didn't answer.

"Michael Jordan used to do this? Put salt in his shoes? Before that he was just a short, white kid?"

Chuck looked at him soberly. "Not white," he said.

"I was kidding," Stan said quickly.

"You aren't supposed to notice race," Chuck blinked.

"I don't, usually. But just for the joke." Stan cleared his throat. "About how tall a fellow are you?"

"I don't know."

"You're shorter than me and I'm short."

Chuck made a face. "But you're a grown up!"

"And I'm a short grown up. All of us in your family are on the short side, which is okay. Nothing wrong with that. Short people live longer, something you'll be hearing for the rest of your life when height is an issue and someone wants to make you feel better. Although frankly when you get to be my age and living those extra years you'll kind of get that the joke was on you the whole time, but let's not worry about that now."

Chuck didn't answer. He shook one shoe distributing the salt then switched to the other.

"All I'm telling you is Grandpa Badge means well but he doesn't know what it's like for guys like you and me. Life isn't all rodeo and camping and wonderland and it's best you learn early that you might not ever be big enough to play basket—"

"You don't know that!" Chuck's lip curled. "You're wrong! You don't know!"

From downstairs Badge called, "Chuck!"

The kid was furious. Without a look back Chuck ran leaving Stan holding the book. The joints in his leg cracked as he rose and stepped over the pile of laundry and into the bathroom across the hall. Toothbrushes lay scattered all around the countertop, studded with gobs of bright green paste. The toilet was running and Stan jiggled the handle, and then on an impulse removed the lid. Gingerly, he reached in and raised the float rod and propped it up with a shampoo bottle. Using a blow-drier on the collar of the overflow pipe, Stan made sure it was dry before taking a gob of petroleum jelly—cringing at the hair and dirt matted to the side of the jar—and slathered the flapper ball hinges. He replaced the porcelain lid and flushed it once. Just a little effort, he muttered out loud. When the water finished recycling he flushed it again and listened to the tinkling of swirling water, and thought about that air conditioner.

STAN TOOK A SECOND DRIVE to Louis's house near dusk, parked his LeSabre a few driveways back, and waited for the house to empty and the ranch caravan to pass by. He opened the trunk, took his green toolbox and approached the house.

The steel condenser unit was bolted to a slab of cement just outside Louis's yard. The shrubs were overgrown and Stan had to break a few juniper twigs before he was able to squat down and get at the bolts. After a few turns he was able to lift the cover on its hinges like an old hat box. He blew at the needles and leaves that had collected and with his flashlight could see the coil was fine, no breaks. The refrigerant piping was in place, the clips holding the compressor to the fan were solid. He was going to have to go inside.

In the velvety purple of early evening, Stan stood dumb at the screen door a moment before it struck him: he wasn't going to be able to get in. He didn't have the keys, Ferrol did. How did he think he was going to get inside without her?

He put his face against the window and looked into the dark room. He was really getting a divorce, really on his own. You couldn't just show up and assume doors would open, that you were welcome. He felt lonely for his own house. Walking back to his car slowly, Stan wished to go to his actual home now, not his recently rented studio but the one he had worked on and lived in for decades. And maybe even have someone in it who loved him.

He didn't notice the body in the driver seat of the LeSabre until he had pulled on the handle and the dome light turned on.

"Sofia! You scared me."

"Leaving so soon, Mr. Overly?"

"Get out of my car," he ordered, resting one hand on the half-lowered window.

"You're a smart guy, Mr. Overly. But maybe a little out of your league when it comes to home invasion."

"I wasn't home invading."

"You need one of these." Sofia opened her hand and held it palm side down where a single brown key dangled from a small chain around her finger like a wedding-ring.

"Where did you get that?"

"What kind of a stalker would I be without a key to the house?"

Stan reached for it but Sofia closed her fist. "I'll let you in."

Stan grunted. "Obviously, Sofia, you aren't allowed in Louis's house."

"That's what you think," she told him, and got out of the car.

Stan tried to copy her nonchalance, striding confidently up the porch, unlocking the door without looking over his shoulder. Once inside he flipped on the light, which Sofia immediately shut back off.

"Not smart," she said removing a small flashlight from her pocket and sweeping the beam across the walls. The heat was intense and Stan was sorry he hadn't changed out of his long sleeves. Even in the moonlight the house looked like it had been left in a hurry: the couches were covered in magazines and toys, clothing was scattered on the floor and backs of chairs.

"He hates the way she keeps house, did you know that?" She reached out and straightened one picture then stood back to examine her work. In the living room she began stacking magazines from the floor on a coffee table. As a gentleman, he looked away to not see her bending over, and immediately bumped into something heavy.

"That's an electronic piano," Sofia told him. "Mom has a beautiful upright under a tarp in the basement that no one is using. She probably would have given it to Louis if he asked, she always liked him so much. Then he wouldn't be stuck with this modern abomination. Listen, it plays the tunes for you. Here's a samba. Want to dance?"

He took a step back as the music started, but she grabbed his arm.

"Come on now, Sofia. We're wasting time."

Swaying gently, her leg brushed against his. He tried to back away but she gripped tightly. "Too stiff," she told him. "Swing those hips." Her body felt warm and coppery, like a malleable element. "Nice," she said. "Better."

He kept his hands away, barely touching her shirt. It had been a long time since he had danced with anyone. Maybe since Louis's wedding. From nowhere came a rush of giddiness: it was crazy to be here in this house with this girl. If he weren't so old or she so young, if he weren't so intent on getting back with his wife. . . . Without warning he dipped Sofia.

She came back up laughing. "You can dance, Mr. Overly. I love a man who can move."

He broke away from her. "I was just being silly," he said defensively. "Turn it off. Let's just do what we came here for."

She put both hands on his cheeks and they touched foreheads. "You want to do what I came here for?" She fluttered her eyes comically.

"I don't know what you came here for," he slipped pulling away from her but she caught him, arms flailing, and he struggled to get out of her grip. "All I'm going to do is have a look at the air conditioner. Are you coming with me?"

"I wouldn't abandon my date just when he got all handy."

He thought to remind her that he wasn't her date, but even to deny it would be admitting that he was playing along on some level. Just a few steps higher the heat was more intense and his clothing tightened around him. Stan pulled the ladder from the ceiling.

The attic was cramped and narrow. Sitting still and somber under the pitch of the roof, was the evaporator unit, silvery air ducts spread around it like lifeless spider legs.

Stan steadied the front plate against his knee to removed it. "Sorry, that smell."

"Mice," Sofia said quietly. She kneeled next to him and pointed her flashlight. Most of the unit was empty with the motor braced against the top. Several dead mice were scattered inside, all in the process of melting.

"You may want to look away," Stan told her.

"I may," Sofia teased, but she didn't. "Why did Mrs. Overly let such a handy guy get away?"

Stan poked around the motor, touching the brackets to see what was causing the rumble. "She left me. She said…. Well and it was sort of true. I did take her for granted some. She thought I stopped making an effort."

"Really?" she asked. "Something as trite as all that? Is it true?"

"Effort is a hard thing to. . . quantify." Insulation, stiff like cotton candy, had gotten caught in the motor and Stan began to remove it by the fistful.

Sofia said, "If it's effort she wants, tell her about this. Fixing a fellow's air conditioning when he isn't even home? That's effort. Of course when she throws herself at you don't go draining your semen supply until I get what I need."

"Sofia Conover," Stan said in his firmest voice possible. He raised himself up on his knees and looked directly at her. "I am a responsible adult and as such, I cannot engage in the activity you're suggesting. We can't even talk about it."

She was going to speak but he held up his hand. "That's enough now. Do you think you could pop down and hit the thermostat?"

"Maybe we could work out a deal where she only gets you when I'm not ovulating."

"The thermostat, Sofia. Now."

She backed away without another word.

The box rumbled to life. He watched the motor chug in the bracket, satisfied. It was done. He had fixed it and having Sofia with him had even been sort of fun. Not that he'd ever act on it, but he did enjoy on some level this new rapport with the girl. It's not like it was even possible to do what she suggested: he'd had a vasectomy years ago. If he really wanted her to go away all he would have to do is mention that.

He felt strange. Why hadn't he told Sofia right away about the vasectomy? Surely that would put an end to all this. And he did want it to end, didn't he?

Once the box had been scraped clean and the cover secure, he found Sofia in the boys room folding an enormous mound of clothes with the light on.

"You did it," she said. "It's cooler already. Louis is really going to be surprised when he gets here on Sunday."

"I want to thank you for your advice. I'm going to see her now, my wife. You've inspired me. I'll just go home and clean off."

"Why do that?" She grunted under a large load of pants going into the bottom bureau drawer. "You should just shower here." She smacked her hands together loudly. "I can show myself out. We've done good work, Mr. Overly."

He waited after hearing the front door close before peeking out the bedroom window and watching Sofia cut across the front lawn and head down the street.

The bathtub had two long sliding smoked glass doors, of which the back one would not slide. Effort was becoming habitual, and after a few nudges, Stan forced the door back into its proper track. He stepped into the shower and gripped the steel safety bar, lined from end to end with shampoo bottles. The bottom of the tub was littered with children's toys, plastic dolphins and mermaids, there was even a little baby seat suction-cupped to the center.

A loud thump on the bathroom door made his legs shake.

"You finally get in there?" It was Sofia. She was in the bathroom.

Stan froze. "You scared me! How did you get in here?"

"Is it even worth asking? I'm getting in with you. How about it?"

"Absolutely not," he yelled. He could see her undressing through the glass. He felt sick to his stomach and reached frantically for bottles trying to find simple shampoo: *silky elixir, aloe, fruity fragrant, relaxing, replenisher*, he squirted a handful of whatever it was into his palm and slapped it on his head. He was vigorously scratching it into his scalp when the lights went out.

"Sofia," he called out quickly. "I changed my mind."

"I thought you might," she said in a coy voice.

"No no! When I was protesting before I was being a little disingenuous. So when I say I changed my mind I mean I really don't want to do this, as opposed to before when I was actually considering it. Get out of the bathroom."

The front panel started to slide but Stan shoved it closed and pressed his weight. "Listen, maybe some other time Sofia," he called. If he admitted his vasectomy now she would wonder why he hadn't mentioned it earlier, and it would be a fair question. "I'm too tired to get the job done tonight, giving you a baby. You really need energy for that."

"Come on now, Mr. Overly. You don't buy that old fashioned notion of the sperm as forceful warrior, do you? The protagonist of the conception drama?" She was pushing so hard on the glass panel that he was afraid he might slip. "You think the egg is just the damsel in distress waiting for the sperm to fight through so she can be passively fertilized?"

"I need you to back off," he said, in his best businesslike voice. "I'm getting out."

She stopped pushing on the door and he relaxed but kept his hands in place on the handle. "Okay. Now let's talk for a second."

The back door slid open; Christ, why had he fixed it? His heart was pounding. He was afraid, he realized, genuinely scared. He moved as far as he could, through the spray, up against the temperature knobs and the tub spigot which poked him in the back of his leg.

"I can't get you pregnant, Sofia."

In the dark her arms and legs seemed elongated shadows reaching for him. Her body was lithe and firm, perfect in the murky light, and he felt ashamed of his old, stumpy body. "Watch out for the toys," he heard himself say.

She took his arm. "The egg actually has a sticky coating and that's what holds the sperm and keeps it from swimming off," she told him calmly. "Tails on sperm really only allow for swimming side to side." She reached down and rubbed his penis. "Something called the zona pellucida, if I'm pronouncing that right, traps the sperm while the egg takes it in and does all the work. The sperm doesn't really do anything other than showing up in the uterus."

Vasectomy, he mumbled. He barely heard it himself. He felt the familiar pressure in his penis. *Not now,* he thought. *Not this soon.*

Sofia said, "Is that what I think it is?" She leaned on him and put her leg on the top of the tub for leverage and stuffed him inside. The spigot dug into his leg like a dull blade. She was everywhere, her hair in his face, her arms clutching his back, and when he exhaled he felt her stomach pressing against his chest.

"I'm not prepared to take you yet but the soap will help. Unless it kills the sperm. Actually it sort of burns. I've got you." She gripped tightly with one hand, squeezing and tugging as if she were milking a cow. The pumping was starting to become painful. But he wasn't actually. . . . He wasn't inside. It hadn't happened.

"It feels like you might be done, here," she said. "You're soft. You mind hopping out and giving me some space to rinse?" She gently pushed him toward the door with her open palm.

Stan stepped out into the cold, bare floor. He felt shriveled and tired. He had tricked her. He had allowed it to happen, could have stopped it at any point, had taken advantage of a poor mentally ill girl for his own sick pleasure, never mind that it hadn't actually been pleasurable.

"Another hilarious element to this whole ritual," she yelled over the water. "Is how lauded men are for the amount of sperm produced in a lifetime. More than a trillion. Great. Most of it ends up as undercoating for computer desks. It's women who should be commended for economical use of our eggs. Three, four pregnancies on average with only 400 eggs to work with." The water turned off and the back door shuttered and stalled.

"Oops . . . I think the door is stuck. Must have come off the runner." She came out the front door and he handed her a towel.

"That went even quicker than I had hoped," she said. "Oh! That doesn't bother you, does it? I like it speedy."

She turned on the lights and Stan looked away rather than watch her dress.

"You'll think I'm crazy of course, but I've got a good feeling about what we did here." She slapped her stomach loudly. "I can all but feel it kicking."

IN THE FOLLOWING DAYS, with much effort, Stan willed himself to put the Sofia "incident" out of his mind, and she helped by not contacting him. But it was a challenge when three days later he found himself summoned to the Conovers by his friend Rupert to help with an emergency furniture move.

"We need the trunk of your LeSabre to carry some smaller crates," Rupert told him on the phone. Stan listened for traces of anger, any clue that he might know about what happened.

Standing in the Conover basement now that it had been emptied of nearly everything gave Stan an agoraphobic queasiness. Spatially, it reminded him of a European train station: a gigantic, impersonal cavern. He was feeling more confident now that his backseat and trunk were full of boxes and he had still not seen Sofia, although he did feel a bit nauseated when he saw the empty space where the bed had been.

"What's next?" Stan absently brushed dust from his pants and sleeves.

"We wait for that juicy tax return to come through from all this donating," Rupert joked. He led Stan to the corner where Beatrice was dusting a wooden bassinette. "Then we're going to open the world's greatest day care center."

Beatrice wheeled around. "Rupert! You're not supposed to tell anyone but.... It's happened, Stan. It's really happening!"

Beatrice threw out her arms and embraced Stan's just as his knees quaked. "We're going to be grandparents!" She pulled away and spoke a few inches from Stan's face. "Please don't tell Ferrol until I get the chance."

"But who's the father?" Stan's voice cracked slightly.

Beatrice looked stung. She looked quickly at Rupert and then back to Stan sharply. "As if it's any of your business!"

"Come on now," Rupert said in a soothing tone. "Steady as she goes, old girl."

"The first thing he says, who's the father?" Beatrice's lip was quivering.

"We don't know yet," Rupert said quietly. "She hasn't told. We're a little concerned considering some of Sofia's past problems."

"I'm not concerned," Beatrice crossed her arms diffidently. "Today's women are smart, women like Sofia. She wanted a baby and she took care of it."

Beatrice's face lit up in triumph as soon as she heard thumping on the stairs. "You want to know so badly," Beatrice challenged Stan. "Why don't you ask her yourself?"

Sofia came down the steps in small, tight jogging shorts and a grey t-shirt. To Stan's horror, the unbidden memory of her pressing hips created a slight twinge in his genitals.

She approached them slowly, looking around the long, empty basement. "You told him, didn't you," she said tightly to her mother.

"Stan promised not to say anything," Beatrice winked. "Did you see this bassinette?"

Sofia's forehead wrinkled, as if working a complicated division problem in her head. "Since Mr. Overly is here," she said quietly. "We might as well do this now."

Stan's low-grade arousal flipped to intense, heart pounding panic.

"This is going to be unpleasant for everyone and won't go down as our best moment."

Rupert stood next to Beatrice who looked unabashedly concerned.

"But you have a right to know. Mr. Overly is the father of my baby."

"That's cruel," Beatrice barked, her sharp voice echoing against the walls. "For shame!"

Stan knitted his brows ambiguously, an expression he hoped resembled dispassionate concern, although it probably looked more like terror.

"We worked out a deal so he won't be involved in raising the baby."

"Shame on you," Beatrice repeated.

"Stan is sterile," Rupert said evenly. "Want to try someone else?"

Sofia rolled her eyes. "Sterile? He's already got one kid in case you've forgotten." She seemed to be just barely putting up with the proceedings.

When Stan finally spoke he felt his stomach drop as if he had jumped from an airplane. "I had a vasectomy." He told her.

Beatrice interjected, "Fifteen years ago at least! Your father and I took them to dinner to celebrate."

Sofia's eyes narrowed fiercely.

"It's true," Stan told her. "You can't be pregnant."

Beatrice looked away from Sofia. "Why couldn't she be pregnant?"

"We're joking, mom," Sofia said quickly. She looked exhausted.

"I knew you were kidding, dear," Rupert said. Both his hands were balled into fists.

Sofia put her hand on Stan's shoulder. "Jay-kay, Mr. Overly."

"That's okay," Stan grunted. "You were only joking about me," he said again.

Her grip tightened like a vice on his shoulder. "I'll be seeing you around," she said, then walked stiffly back up the stairs.

HE HAD FALLEN ASLEEP with the television on and woke to the sound of a woman's voice on a commercial. He began shrieking, sure Sofia was in the apartment baring down on him with a knife. He made a cup of tea to calm down and drank it with all the lights on. Right after Ferrol asked him to leave and he had moved into his studio, Stan cheered himself by planning to invite his buddies over for dinner. He imagined them laughing and slapping each other on their backs while watching Stan working in his kitchen, orange flames searing the bottom of a skillet as he flipped some complicated dish into the air. Now he couldn't think of a single "buddy" he might invite over, let alone three of them. Plus, the burners on the stove were electric.

He was just getting back into bed when the intercom buzzed. His throat was dry. "Yes?"

"It's me."

"Sofia. I'm in bed, in my pajamas because it's so late. Let's talk about this later."

Sofia Conover is not a person to cross, he remembered Louis saying something similar years and years ago on the occasion of discovering yet another penetrated security door at his office. Someone had gone in with large rubber tubs and sorted years worth of advertising copy and invoices. The police never proved who had done it and Louis was still using her system.

"Buzz me in, Overly."

"We should talk about this," he said. "I did a terrible thing to you and I apologize. But let's do this in public." This was straight from the pamphlet: if the stalker confronts you, move at once to a public place. He didn't know if the advice applied if the stalker wasn't technically stalking *you*, but it still seemed like a wise choice.

"Sofia?" he said to the grill. He strained to listen: the eerie hiss of nothing. He put his ear on the intercom. The pounding on his door made him jump.

"I'm right outside, Mr. Overly. You don't have to be afraid. The most I might do is slap you once, and I'm pretty sure I won't even do that."

"Shhhh," he pleaded. He slid the bolt and opened the door.

She took a quick step in and suddenly struck him across his face. Stan rocked back, stunned. He held out his arms to grab something and she reached for him and steadied his flailing body, tilting forward then back as if they were dancing again.

"Sorry," she said roughly. "Sorry. I was pretty sure that wasn't going to happen. I think I cut you with my watchband."

Stan wiped his face and winced at the blood on the back of his hand. "I'm so sorry, Sofia," he was speaking as quickly as possible. "I took advantage."

She flung him back and he teetered a few seconds before deliberately lowering himself to the carpet. He was cowering the way dogs did it, right? Indicated supplication to the alpha by laying down?

Sofia stomped into his kitchen. Stan heard her roughly opening and closing cabinet doors, slamming some of the drawers. He couldn't see over the counter, but when he raised himself slightly he could just see the top of her hair.

"What I did was incorrigible," he said gulping quickly. "I took advantage and I'm sorry." She came out of the kitchen with a several ice cubes balled into a paper towel. "Put this on your lip." She leaned down to place the ice on the injury, but at the last second she struck him with it, two fast shots right on the swelling before he could get his arms up to stop her.

"Sofia! Sofia!"

"All right," she said at last. She placed the ice on his face and he took it. "It's out of my system now."

He sat up against his bed and to his surprise she sat next to him. She reached out for the ice bag but he yanked it away.

"Let me see," she said almost tenderly. "That's going to look terrible. Keep ice on it."

"Sofia," he began. "I know that a woman wants to have a baby at a certain point in her life, but this plan of yours really wasn't the best way to go about having one."

She chortled dryly. "That's an understatement."

"And really, Sofia. It's for the best that you didn't get pregnant."

"Oh?"

"Absolutely. You could adopt. They let single moms do it all the time and the churches have lots of ways to *persuade* mothers in poor countries to hand over their children."

"That would have been a good solution. Only thing, I'm already pregnant."

"Now, Sofia. No you aren't."

"Yes I am," she said. "Nearly six weeks."

He took the ice off his lips. He understood now. It was painful for a moment, much worse than the lip, but at the same time it was a relief.

She continued, "I was trying to spare the actual father. He's married and has another family."

"I was a patsy," Stan said at last. He put his tongue on his lip and felt the throbbing. "A patsy. Why did you pick me?" he mumbled. "Of all the chumps on the planet, why me?"

Her shoulder rubbed against his as she shrugged. "To establish.... plausible paternity. The baby's going to look like you, like an Overly. Louis. He's the father."

Stan blinked at her, momentarily stupefied.

Sofia sighed wearily. "Congratulations, Mr. Overly. You're going to be a grandfather. Again."

WHEN THE NEWS BROKE, Stan let his answering machine field all the calls. The hasty message from Louis saying he had some news and Stan should call back. Ferrol asking if he had heard anything and please call back. Rupert just wanting to talk so call back when convenient. Stan deleted them as they came in and stayed in his studio keeping his head down.

A strong desire to see his house finally lured him back into the LeSabre. The single-story brick craftsman he and Ferrol owned was brown and red with a screened porch and a deck in the back overlooking a long yard. Though he hadn't been here in many months, he had to admit Ferrol was doing an adequate job keeping it up. The stone walk was swept and whomever she was paying to maintain the lawn had kept it a thick three inches.

Before he could ring the bell a thumping noise from behind the house caught his attention, so he walked around to the back. On the cement patio where Ferrol used to keep feeders and a bird bath, a basketball net on a steel post had been erected. Under it was Chuck, lunging from side to side, furiously bouncing the ball in front of him. He looked more like a dancer than a ball player.

Stan felt a thrill at seeing the boy. He sprinted across the yard to the patio waving and calling, "Chuck! Chucky! Boy!"

Chuck cocked to take another shot but stopped. His jaw hung open as Stan approached, not in surprise, exactly, but more like a dull sort of confusion. Stan stretched his arms but thought better of hugging the boy when he saw the amount of perspiration in his hair.

"Throw me the ball, Chuck!" Stan planted his legs. "I'll show you how to take a shot. Bounce it to me, boy! Bounce it to me."

Chuck grinned fiercely. He was short but sinewy, and he held the ball above his head and hurled it, all biceps and bared teeth. Stan lunged for the ball but it smacked against his face and he found himself knocked to the ground, sprawled on his elbows and back.

"Good God, Stan. Are you okay?" It was Ferrol. She came running from the deck to where Stan lay. "Where did you come from? What happened?"

"He did that on purpose!" Stan huffed, struggling to sit up.

Chuck hadn't moved to help him. He pushed his curly hair out of his eyes, his mouth in the same slack position. Chuck seemed pretty tall now in those shorts and that tank top, the figure of an athlete.

"But that's okay," Stan called out to the boy. He tried to stand but his foot throbbed sharply. "That's okay. You hear me Chuck? I'm not mad at you. You taught me a pretty good lesson there." With Ferrol's help he struggled to his feet.

"What on Earth were you doing out there?" she asked. She let Stan lean heavily and walked him up the deck.

"You look nice," he told her instead of answering. He wanted to say more, that she was beautiful, but didn't know how to begin to say it without acknowledging that he should have said it long ago. She didn't have her glasses on, nothing to break up her face; a sweet, upturned nose and prominent cheekbones and large eyes, which, though the skin around them had loosened were still as pretty as they'd ever been. In fact, he supposed it had now been three or four months since actually seeing her face, which made him momentarily reel with misery.

"Sit," she told him in the kitchen. Her head disappeared into the freezer.

Stan settled himself on a warm kitchen chair. It was going to rain soon. He hadn't known that outside, but in the house he could tell the way the wood felt beneath his feet, the way the hinge on the cabinet had creaked. He rolled his pant leg and rested his foot across another chair. He turned the corner of a book on the kitchen table, a fresh baby book, along with a collection of her fancy calligraphy pens.

"That was going to be for the new baby. You see I have to buy a new book because I made a mistake," she fitted a soft ice pack around his ankle. "I put Melody's parents in the family tree. Force of habit."

Stan nodded. "It must be hard on Melody."

Ferrol sat across from him and took his foot in her lap. "It's a nightmare for her. For everyone. Louis too, that idiot. He's caused a lot of pain. Of course the Conovers are thrilled, the baby isn't going to lack for anything. Sofia and Melody are even going to make an effort to be friendly. Hopefully the baby will feel like it has two families, one with lots of brothers and sisters, and one with a mom where it gets undivided attention."

"Makes you realize how important that stuff is, families staying together." To not acknowledge the look she gave him, he quickly added, "When did the basketball court go up?"

"You really haven't been here in awhile, have you?"

"Wasn't sure what I'd do if I did come."

"Well," Ferrol continued to rub his foot. "The robins are nesting again in the bathroom vent. You could start there and then maybe see if anything else needs work. If you're willing to work, that is."

Stan nodded, suddenly not wanting to hear the sound of his own voice. He looked away from her, looked out the window where he could see Chuck fighting off invisible blockers, feinting and weaving, leaping into the air and firing off a shot. The ball's bounce off the rim didn't seem to matter to Chuck, who threw his arms in the air and leapt up and down furiously, shadow dancing some future victory.

Under the Nazarene Sun

Because Jesus was born with no arms, he relied on his mother (Mary) to do the things that others in Nazareth did for themselves. She bathed him, soaped him up and rinsed him off, shampooed and combed his long hair, trimmed his beard with toe-nail scissors and used a damp rag to clean his neck and behind his ears. She dressed him every morning, pulling his shirt over his head, bunching up the legs of his jeans so he could more easily step into them, buttoned his fly and buckled his sandals. She prepared all his food and fed him, alternating one fork-full for him, one for herself. She patted him down in the evenings with Skin So Soft so that the bugs wouldn't eat at him, since he didn't have arms to swat them away.

Even into his thirties, she kept Jesus in diapers and changed him twice a day, she cleaned his front and bottom with baby wipes, and kept his flesh tender with cocoa butter. Occasionally her knuckles would brush against the hairs on his buttocks and testicles, and this tickled Jesus. He liked the feeling it gave him, a funny itch, and sometimes he twitched or jerked deliberately so that Mary's hand would brush against those sensitive parts.

At night, after pulling his burlap blanket up to his chin with his mouth, Jesus would think about these brief accidental contacts, and feel itchy again. He would turn over in his bed and rub himself against the palmated leaves and dried corncobs in his mattress. But no matter how hard he rubbed and abraded his skin, the itch never disappeared for long.

Although Jesus had no arms, he did have hands at the ends of his shoulders. These hands were equipped with five little protrusions, which looked more like the teats of a nursing sow than fingers, but they had joints and could move. By contorting his body and nudging objects with the protrusions, he could grab and even hold things.

His mind worked on solutions towards overcoming his handicap. "If I took a reed from the bank of the Jordan, and fastened to this reed one cone from a pine tree," he thought. "I would have a right handy toothbrush." But he never shared these thoughts with his mother. He liked the way she manipulated the brush in his mouth, the way she rested one arm on his shoulder while sweeping his teeth back and forth, the gentle nudge for him to bend and spit into the sink. He enjoyed the intimacy that complete dependance gave them.

In the afternoons, Jesus went often to the Tenderloin district to hang with the street people and watch the whores. Because of his severe handicap, the spectacular visualness of it, Jesus knew he could make quite a bit of money begging on the street. But he had been cautioned against this by his mother who considered begging shameful—especially, as she pointed out, since she had a good job and they weren't hurting for money.

But Jesus became smitten with one of the whores, one with brown hair and dark lashes, and long lean legs like his mother. She would smile at him and once even offered half a bagel that she was eating.

Jesus knew where his mother kept her "mad money," and one morning, after she left for work, he took some. He stooped down at an angle so he could use his finger to push aside her panties and stockings until he came across a roll of bills with a rubber band around it. By leaning left and right alternately, Jesus worked at the rubber band and removed a few bills; nothing she would ever notice, just enough to get an afternoon with the whore.

Her name was Mary, like his mother, and she had a kind soft voice like his mother too. She was surprised to see Jesus at her door that afternoon. She remembered him from the neighborhood and knew him to be a *mensch*.

"You've never been with a woman?" she asked.

Jesus gritted his teeth, trying not to blush, but he could feel it was hopeless.

"Oh, you're such a dear. And you want me to be the first?"

He opened his fingers and the crumpled ball of bills dropped to the floor. The breeze on his palms made him realize how clammy they were, and he rubbed them against his shoulders to dry them.

"You have such nice hair," Mary told him, and came around back and began to brush it. Jesus watched her in a mirror that covered most of the opposite wall. She smelled of cigarette butts and maple syrup, and she began to braid his hair and hum a cloying tune in his ear. Jesus wished she would finish this part, the foreplay or whatever it was, and get to the good stuff. But he didn't say anything because he was used to these feelings: calm patience, helplessness, waiting for someone to finish what they wanted to do before remembering his needs.

"I'm jealous of your mother, in a way, Jesus," Mary whispered to him. "I can't have a baby because they put a stone in my uterus to keep me from getting pregnant. Now I'll never have a little boy like you, to take care of and watch over. She's lucky to still be so close to you, even if it's just because you're deformed."

When she had braided his mane down to the last inch and tied a little red ribbon on the tip, she sighed and rested her freckled arms on his shoulder. He watched her head in the mirror as she whispered into his ear.

"You know what? I don't think I'm going to be able to go through with this."

Jesus lowered his eyes to ground, and exhaled through tight lips.

"I don't see it happening," Mary continued. "After you mounted me you wouldn't be able to hump. I could hold you in position by your hips, but I don't have the strength to thrust for you."

Jesus cleared his throat. "You could get on top of me, hold on to my neck maybe; or you could use a bedpost if we were on an angle, and use that as leverage."

"I'd be sliding all over the place."

"If there was a wooden bar that I could clutch, something to hold up here," he wiggled his fingers. "You could hang on to this bar and if you didn't yank too hard—"

"No, no. I would feel too restrained. Besides, a woman needs her face slapped to make love, and her hair yanked at just the right times. So I don't think it's going to happen. But I tell you what; I can do something else for you."

She pressed herself against his back and put her arms forward so that his fingers rested on her shoulders. She dropped her arms to his side.

"Look Jesus, this is how a real man looks."

He saw himself in the mirror. She was hiding behind his head, and he could hear her breathing and feel her heat. But in the mirror he saw only himself, a man with long, freckled arms. She slowly moved her hands so that her palms were on his stomach.

"This is how a man shows that he's enjoyed a meal."

She rubbed his belly and then patted it with her fingers.

"Mmmm, that was good," she said. "Say mmmmm, Jesus."

"Yum," he said, and her hands patted his stomach. "That was a delicious dinner, mom." He puffed his belly out and she dropped her hands to the underside and grabbed his paunch roughly. "I couldn't eat another bite!" Jesus cried.

Her fingers dug in and Jesus watched himself, a contented, well-fed, whole man. He actually felt full, and he craned his neck and gave a hearty yawn.

"And this is how a man thinks," Mary said into his ear.

She brought her arms up and around his head. She touched his cheek with one finger and cupped his chin with her other hand.

"Hmmmm," she said. "I'm thinking something deeply. Think with me, Jesus."

She tapped his lip pensively and he murmured, "Hmmm. . . ." He furled his eyebrows and the skin on his forehead lined. She crossed one arm over his chest, her other finger stroked his beard.

A grin appeared through his thoughtful expression, but just for a second, and he continued playing. "What was . . . that man's name . . . that I'm trying to think of. . . ."

"Check your phone book, Jesus." She pantomimed a book in front of him with one hand and stuck her finger to his lip. "Lick the tip."

He licked her finger and then watched himself turning the pages of the book.

"Wow," he said.

"I'm wiping the sweat off my brow," she said and rubbed his forehead. He watched himself flick the sweat off his hands into the air.

"I'm scratching my armpit," she said. "I'm hiking my trousers up. I'm adjusting my package. I'm scratching my nose."

And thus Jesus watched himself in the mirror do all the things a man can do. "I'm pulling my hair," he called out. "I'm rubbing my eyes. I'm stroking my beard. I'm checking my pockets. I'm cracking my knuckles." And Jesus stood and moved his arms like any man, and he extended them, stretched his arms as far as he could. He took in the bed and the mirror and the whole of Mary's room. And he knew that soon he would stand in the middle of the city, and his arms would grow to encompass it entirely, every building and every person would disappear in his arms and feel his embrace and they would know his name.

ON THE DAY OF HIS CRUCIFIXION, Jesus was dismayed to see that he was causing one headache after another for the centurions. Right off the bat there had been a terrible argument between the two men who had come for him over whether or not Jesus needed to be handcuffed. The older centurion with the beard had pointed out that Jesus, not having arms, made handcuffing fairly pointless. But the young one, who still wore the patch on his chest indicating he was a rookie, insisted that the regulations were unambiguous that each prisoner be handcuffed. It was Jesus himself who, in an effort to diffuse the tension between the men, suggested that they use the handcuffs on his ankles, thereby fulfilling the letter of the law.

And in the park where the prisoners were being nailed to crosses in numerical order, Jesus posed an even greater problem. At first they tried just nailing his feet even though Jesus tried a number of times to tell them that wouldn't work. And sure enough, the second the slack had gone out of the lead rope, and the cross had been hoisted into place, Jesus—trying to be a good sport and holding his body erect—swung like a pendulum, his head inches over the fresh sod.

The group of soldiers responsible for his section rushed forward. The dilemma had caught the attention of the Line Supervisor and the Section Head, and both marched officiously towards the crowd. The dangling prisoner now swung gently from his ankles.

"I hate to say this, but I told you so," Jesus said humbly.

"Now what are we going to do?" one of the men asked the Line Supervisor.

The Line Supervisor looked at his clipboard, which held all the work-order documents for the afternoon. He was slightly irritated at having this hitch occur while he was being watched by the Section Head; but this was a golden opportunity to show he could think on his feet and put out fires if he needed to. He flipped a few pages on his clipboard and pursed his lips, before realizing this was the exact wrong posture to strike. He needed to come up with something that wasn't in the regs, his own solution. "Hmmmm," he said, trying to appear thoughtful.

"You could leave me like this," Jesus offered. "It's very painful, and I'll be dead soon."

"That's true," mused the Line Supervisor.

"But then it's not a crucifixion," the Section Head said stepping forward. He was disappointed at his Line Supervisor.

One of the Crucifixion Technicians cleared his throat. "His head will fill with blood," he said tentatively, rubbing his thumb over the head of his mallet. "It'd eventually burst like an over-ripe plum."

"It's unorthodox," another Tech—a shorter man— jumped in. He wanted the Section Head to notice him too. "Although, it would carry out the spirit of the edict." He wrinkled his face in the pensive way he had seen the Line Supervisor adopt when pretending to think.

"Nonsense!" The Section Head was astonished to see the cavalier attitude of this whole department. How had he given all the hiring power over to his ineffectual Line Supervisor, who clearly did not respect the Operational Procedures? He would take over this whole work-order, and then see about filing a carefully worded report to his Manager. "Let's start brainstorming here."

"You could use one more nail," Jesus said. The others looked down towards Jesus' face. He had stopped swaying and the long hairs of his mangy beard were obscuring his mouth and nose. Jesus pressed his lips together and spit some hairs away from his mouth. "Maybe you could stake me through my chest or neck," he suggested.

There was some general nodding and quiet murmuring, which stopped dead when the Section Head said, "No. That might kill you. The OP states crucifixion must be the cause of death."

"Well, how about if you braid my hair into a rope, and tie it to the cross?"

The men looked up, considering it for a moment. They betrayed nothing to each other by way of expression.

"Could work," the Section Head said slowly. The men began to nod. "One nail up top and one on bottom. It's not classic crucifixion, but would get the job done."

"What if we tie him around the waist too," the Line Supervisor said enthusiastically. He knew he had lost some ground with his boss and was eager to get back in his good graces. "Or maybe we could get a bungee cord and strap it across his chest for a little more support."

"And for insurance," the shorter Technician jumped in, "the prisoner could clench his butt cheeks together and hold himself in place against the cross."

"I'm willing to try," Jesus said.

The Section Head beamed at the Technician. "A terrific idea," he said.

The Line Supervisor felt an acute desire to regain control of the situation, he couldn't afford to have one of his own Technicians promoted over him. "Okay," he barked. "Get him down from there and find someone to braid his hair. And let's use the crown of thorns too. Maybe no one will notice the braids."

BECAUSE JESUS DID NOT WANT to inflict more worry on the men who were crucifying him, he struggled to keep his good posture on the cross. But he suffered greatly for this, the thick twine dug into his chest, and his knees trembled.

Snakes of sweat poured off his face, but he was used to not being able to fan himself; in this way, he was better equipped to handle the long afternoon than others on their crosses. "Mighty hot," one man muttered. Jesus looked over and nodded, but the man was talking to himself and didn't notice.

It was nearly dusk and the sun was setting behind the crucified men when the centurions finished raising all the crosses, and began packing up the equipment. The smaller Technician walked over to Jesus and cocked his head, inspecting the job one last time. "You holding up?" he called out.

Jesus began an answer but found his throat and lips so dry that no sound would emerge. Instead he winked and grinned at the man, who gave a shy smile back, and then left.

Jesus looked down at the base of the cross and followed the line of shadow that bisected the park. He saw himself as the shadow of that cross, rising up over all of Nazareth. Even as the sun dropped still lower behind him, his wooden arms stretched to embrace the entire swirl of humanity at his front: the families finishing their picnics and picking up their litter, the shoeshine boys leaving their posts, the mall-walkers pausing now to check their pulses, snack vendors rolling their carts away, tee-shirt vendors boxing up remainders, the low rumble of an L Train shook somewhere in the distance. And all the while the sun continued to set and his arms continued to grow, stretching up and beyond the city; his arms reached townhouses, duplexes, whole subdivisions, into the country and across prairies. With arms like these there were no hearts he could not touch, no faces he could not caress, no lands he could not survey and then raze and then reconstruct. His arms grew and grew, racing against the darkness, reaching another city and then another; each one swallowed into a promise, a distinct and concrete promise, whispered in the faint umbra of stretching limbs, a promise kept until moon replaces sun.

Acknowledgments

Thanks to the editors of the following publications, where versions of these stories originally appeared: *The Baffler*, *The Beloit Fiction Review*, *Oxford Magazine*, *Chicago Center for Literature and Photography Weekender*, *Fifth Wednesday Journal*, and *Santa Monica Review*.

I am deeply grateful to the amazing staff at Cornerstone Press: Dr. Ross Tangedal, Allison Lange, Sophie McPherson, Eva Nielsen, and Ava Willett. Working with them has been a joy.

Thank you to Robert Pollard and Guided by Voices for the song, "Shocker in Gloomtown," and a thousand others.

Lastly, thanks to Molly, Ben, and Madeleine. They know why.

Dan Libman lives on a farm in northern Illinois, where he collects eggs and sneaks food to the barn cats. His work has appeared in many lit journals. He is the author of two previous volumes of fiction: *Book of Grudges* (2023) and *Married but Looking* (2011).